The
BILLIONAIRE
Soulmates

PETRA NICOLL

The Billionaire Soulmates

Published by Duende Press
www.duendepressbooks.com

ISBN-13: 978-0-9915254-4-7

CHAPTER ONE

BLISS

Eli Evans rooted his head firmly against the seatback of a plush recliner in his Boeing 722 jet. He was used to sleeping on planes. Just five more hours and he and the band would be landing in Bangkok; he wanted to get some shuteye now to make it easier to adjust to the time change.

The chamomile tea the flight attendant had prepared for him would help him relax. The guys gave him shit for it, but he didn't care. It worked.

It was late October, and this would be their last gig before taking a two-month break over the holidays. It was a new rule Eli had insisted upon—he wanted everyone on the crew to have the opportunity to be with their families. He had an ulterior motive as well. A sweet smile graced his lips as he allowed memories of the past few weeks to caress him to sleep.

"Mr. Eli?" A gentle tap on his shoulder jarred him awake. "I'm sorry, Mr. Eli, but the plane will be landing shortly." *Already?* Eli thought, a bit begrudgingly because he'd been just about to climax in his dream. Maybe it was for the best; if he'd moaned out loud, the guys would never have let him hear the end of it.

"Okay. Thank you, Nin," he addressed the young Thai flight attendant with a nod. He glanced over at his bass player, Jimbo, who was making googly eyes at Nin. "Hey, Jimbo," Eli threw a pillow at his head. "Try not to drool," he whispered when Nin was out of earshot.

"Hey, a man can look, can't he?"

Eli grinned. He loved his band. They were good guys. A little quirky perhaps, a little testosterone-filled, definitely. But they were clean (he prohibited any drug use besides marijuana), honest, and hard workers. He kept them on hectic schedules during touring and recording seasons, but he also rewarded them handsomely—not just with money, but with well-deserved time off.

After this gig, he hoped to have many more moments like the one he'd just dreamed about. *Two months of bliss*, he thought. He still couldn't believe Angelina had agreed to date him again. He thought he'd lost her forever after their competing schedules had kept them from having the time to commit to their relationship earlier that year. *I wasn't ready for her then anyway*, he admitted.

After their breakup, Eli had spent the entire following year at his secluded property in the Bahamas—meditating, practicing yoga, eating healthy, writing new material, and... remaining celibate. He couldn't believe he'd survived the latter. But, he understood that last component was probably the most critical to his having reached a heightened state of creativity.

"The point of this experience is to limit distractions," Michael had told him. Eli chuckled at the memory. *And that son of a bitch was right*, he laughed.

Michael was always right, Eli knew. If it hadn't been for him, who knows where he'd be today. *Probably dead,* he thought. *If I hadn't intentionally killed myself, the road would have found some way to do it for me.*

As the pilot expertly landed the jet, Eli let out a sigh of relief. That moment always put him a bit on edge. It wasn't death itself that scared him—Michael's lessons about reincarnation taught him not to fear death—it was the fear of dying before he'd finished fulfilling this life's purpose.

Come to think of it, I haven't heard from Michael in a while, Eli thought. *I must be doing everything right,* a faint glimpse of ego surfaced in his mind. Just then, a loud crash made him jolt. He turned around. "I'm so sorry, Mr. Eli. Sorry, sorry. I don't know what happened." Nin began to pick up the items that had fallen off the food and drink cart.

Eli shrugged his shoulder and collected his jacket and duffel bag. The porter would take care of the rest.

THE HOT BANGKOK air greeted him as he exited the airport. It didn't take long before the shirt he was wearing became drenched in sweat. An old Indian driver stood leaning against a white Tesla limousine at curbside pickup. "Mr. Evans, right this way," he directed Eli and the other band members to the open door. Eli's manager, Russ, greeted the driver, "Good evening, Ashok. Nice to see you again."

The old man nodded. "The pleasure is mine, sir." Eli didn't remember the driver, but nonetheless, he felt oddly familiar to him. He was impressed that his manager remembered his name. Then again, it was his job to coordinate all the details of the tour, and he did so with great detail.

"To the Grand Palace Hotel, yes?" the driver asked. "Yes, that's correct," Russ answered.

Eli inhaled deeply and slowly released his breath as he watched the busy city streets go by. He couldn't wait to slow down after that night's gig. He'd finally get to enjoy the new property he'd picked out with Angelina at Carbon Beach near Malibu, California. It had instantly felt like home to both of them. *I can't believe I'm doing this*, he thought.

It would be the first time he'd moved in with a woman. Between Angelina's acting schedule and his touring schedule, making time for each other had remained difficult after they reunited. They decided that moving in together might ease some of that strain.

Eli's commitment anxiety gave way to excitement at the thought of waking up next to her day after day. They each had taken the next two months off to enjoy each other's company…*without distractions*, he laughed. Michael would be proud. He would be far from celibate this time around, but he'd done the work. He could enjoy her body all he wanted now; he'd already cleansed his body and mind and acknowledged his soul. *She is my soulmate*, he smiled.

The limo pulled up to the hotel entrance. *Chic*, Eli thought as he looked up at the nineteen-story building. He was sure he'd have the penthouse suite, as always. Those things didn't impress him much, but nonetheless, the venue host for every gig his manager booked insisted that he have the best room at the best hotel in town.

Eli Evans, rock star extraordinaire, he laughed at the thought. Yes, he made billions of dollars—through his music, and through his numerous business endeavors and investments—but he had not forgotten his humble farm roots in Brownsville, Oregon. *Besides, I probably give more money away than I make these days*, he realized proudly.

Since having his awakening—with Michael's assistance—Eli understood his soul's purpose. Or at least, he thought he did. It was an ongoing journey during which he'd occasionally stray from his path and need to be guided back on. But one thing was certain—he'd learned the importance of giving back. He'd initiated countless philanthropic endeavors since returning from the Bahamas. A portion of every performance fee went directly to charity. He became an avid spokesperson for causes dear to his heart.

His emphasis now was on children in India—where Angelina's father was from. He'd learned about the desperate conditions children in the slums were raised in, within walls right up against the wealthiest neighborhoods in the country. Angelina had starred in a film about the topic, *The People on the Other Side*, which was responsible for their reconnecting. On a whim, he'd bought a ticket to its premiere at a film festival in L.A. after returning from the Bahamas. He could not have been more surprised—or excited—to discover Angelina not only in the film but there in person.

I can't believe I asked her out in front of hundreds of people in the audience, he recalled with a grin. His one shot at speaking with her directly was through a microphone during the after-show Q&A. Thankfully, she'd said yes. They went out for a late dinner that night, but he was so nervous he could hardly eat. After being isolated on an island for so long (and on a no-sex diet), just looking at her made him excited. When she touched his arm? He knew it was over. He had to have her. She felt it, too.

She could sense the change in him. They talked for hours about what he'd been through over the past year—how he'd reconnected with his parents, cleaned up his diet ("You're a vegetarian now?!" she'd laughed in delight), maintained a daily meditation and yoga practice, and had incorporated new elements into his music. He'd hesitated at first, but eventually, he even told her about Michael.

"Do you have a guru or something?" she'd asked, incredulous at the changes in him.

"Well…not a guru. He calls himself a guide."

"Uh huh." Angelina smiled knowingly but did not press him for details.

"His name is Michael. He's become a great friend," Eli held her gaze, deciding how much he wanted to reveal. "Actually, I don't see him all that often anymore."

"Teachers enter our lives when we need them," she grinned.

"Exactly," he smiled back at her. God, she was beautiful.

Eli made his way up to the nineteenth floor of the Bangkok hotel. *Such a large room for one person*, he thought. Champagne and strawberries were elegantly displayed on a tray table. He popped a strawberry into his mouth but ignored the champagne. It was a rare occasion when he enjoyed an alcoholic beverage nowadays, and he didn't even miss it.

It was two o'clock in the afternoon, local time. Just enough time to take a shower, change, and get ready for sound check. The concert venue was a few blocks away. He had just finished his shower when he was caught off guard by a knock on the door.

"Who is it?" he called through the door.

"We are your massage therapists, sir."

Massage therapists? he thought. *I didn't ask for that. Perhaps Russ ordered me a massage? He's never done that before, though*, he pondered.

He wrapped a towel around his waist and opened the

door.

"Sorry, just got out of the shower," he took in the two young Thai girls before him. And they were, indeed young. One of them couldn't have been older than twelve, although she was dressed in high heels and wore makeup. "I didn't order a massage," he stated.

"You are Mr. Parker, no?" the oldest girl replied.

"No, I believe you have the wrong room."

The girls looked embarrassed. "So sorry, sir. We will look into our mistake." The girls bowed and made their way swiftly down the hall.

That was strange, Eli thought, as he closed and locked the door. The experience was a bit unsettling, but he pushed it aside in order to focus on preparing for his show that night. A few minutes later, there was another knock on the door.

"Eli," his manager's voice came through the door. "The limo is out front. The guys are already there."

"Got it, thanks Russ. I'll be right down." Eli took one last look at himself in the mirror. His blonde hair had gotten curlier with age, although he was only twenty-six years old. His hazel eyes revealed his youthful spirit, and his slender but muscular build made it clear he took good care of his body. He worked with a personal trainer three days per week, but he believed it was his daily yoga practice that was ultimately responsible for the strength he'd acquired over the past year.

"Go get 'em," he told his reflection in the mirror, before stepping inside the private elevator that would carry him to the first floor.

Going home after Bangkok was extra sweet. From the

airport, he drove his Aston Martin straight to Carbon Beach. When he arrived at the oceanfront property it was after dark. He passed through the security gate, parked, and paused before entering the home; he wanted to soak in the moment. Through the grand front window, he could see Angelina. She was unpacking boxes, listening to music and singing along.

"I'm such a lucky guy," he said aloud to himself. Suddenly, she became aware of his presence. She smiled and rushed to open the door.

"Ah! Welcome home!" she threw herself into his open arms. Any words he might have issued in response were rendered mute by their long, passionate kiss. Eli kicked the door shut with his foot, lifted her up as she straddled his waist, and carried her to the couch. It was overflowing with empty boxes, but as one hand held her up by her bottom, the other flung the boxes onto the floor.

He gently lowered her down. *My God, that ass,* he thought as his hands squeezed and stroked and finally slapped one cheek.

"Ah!" she cried out, but from pleasure. It had been a long time since he'd ravaged her like this, and she liked it. She desperately wanted him inside of her. She unbuckled his belt and threw it to the floor as he bit her neck. Eli unbuttoned his own shirt and added it to the pile of clothes that was accumulating on the floor.

Angelina had been wearing yoga pants, but those had been the first thing to go. His hands wandered up her t-shirt and found her breasts, which he was so glad were rarely blocked by a bra. He liked them like this; raw and ripe. His mouth encapsulated her nipple as she arched her back and quietly moaned.

"No one can hear us here," Eli whispered. He lowered his face down between her legs and circled his tongue around her clitoris and the folds of her labia. She allowed herself to cry out. When she was dripping wet, he raised his body and looked her in the eye.

"I love you," he spoke softly. "Do you want me inside of you?"

"I do," she nodded and held his gaze as he entered her softly, slowly. They joined rhythm and breath in unison, like a dance.

"I missed you," Eli whispered.

"I love you," Angelina replied.

Eli grinned like a schoolboy as he sank in deeper.

In order to optimize their vacation time together, Eli had insisted on hiring both a housekeeper and a chef for the days they were at home. Although he had adapted comfortably to a more holistic, vegetarian diet while in the Bahamas, he made exceptions while on the road. He wanted to get back in the habit of juicing and eating strictly vegetarian and he knew the surest way to do so was by having someone else prepare his meals.

He could be lazy, he admitted. And he could be swayed by temptation. Just the other night, he had been out to dinner with Angelina at a restaurant when the scent of fried pork wafted toward their table from the kitchen.

"I…I'm thinking about having a burger tonight. With bacon." Eli felt like he was making a confession to a priest.

"Okay," Angelina replied without missing a beat.

"Wait…just okay?" Eli looked at her suspiciously. "You just made that whole speech after reading John Robbins' *Diet for a New America*. Remember? You were so upset about the inhumane conditions and the suffering animals endure that you were in tears. You were convinced that the root of most disease is the use of pesticides, hormones, and chemicals used in the production of meat products. You said human consumption of meat was the cause of our planet's ecological crisis."

"I remember."

"I'm confused. Why don't you care that I'm going to order meat then?"

"I do care. But it's your body and your choice. If I tell you what to do or not do, you will resent me later. I prefer for you to answer for yourself what is best for you or not."

"Okay…" *That makes sense*, Eli thought. *Angelina is so different than any other girl I've dated.*

He contemplated what to order. Damn, he wanted that burger. But he also remembered how he'd felt the last time he ate a burger after having gone through a cleanse. He'd been on the toilet for what felt like hours. Was it worth it? Suddenly, the scent he inhaled didn't smell as great.

"What are you having?"

"The kale salad with quinoa," Angelina replied.

"I'll have that, too."

Angelina smiled.

For the next two months, the couple passed their days with morning meditation and yoga on the beach, swimming, making love, and making music. Eli hadn't known Angelina was musically inclined. He discovered that she sang and played the harmonium like an angel.

They also talked for hours—about dreams, intentions, and ideas for songs and screenplays. If it were true that Eli needed to abstain from sex in order to sharpen his creativity the year before, this time around being completely in love did the trick. With Angelina, he felt unstoppable.

WHEREAS THE TWO spent a quiet Thanksgiving alone at their new home, as Christmas approached, Eli was certain where they needed to be.

"What do you think about…meeting my parents?" Eli had asked her hesitantly. Even though they'd already moved in together, he was concerned she'd fear they were moving too fast.

"I thought you'd never ask," she wrapped her arms around his neck and kissed him. "I can't wait to meet the two souls who created *this* beautiful soul."

"You flatter me."

"Would you prefer I disgrace your good name?" Angelina asked playfully. "*Eli Evans, sponsor of raw, vegan café, seen contemplating ordering a burger*," she laughed.

"I wouldn't be surprised if that headline showed up in the news. The paparazzi has been relentless lately," Eli sighed, suddenly feeling serious.

"I know," Angelina's tone matched his. "It is exhausting. It's like having Big Brother watching us 24/7, twisting every move we make into a criminal offense."

Silence enveloped the room as Angelina decided to ask about something that had been bothering her.

"Eli?"

"Yes?"

"I read something last month that…well, I'm sure it isn't true, but still, I just want to ask you about it."

"Sure, go ahead." Eli felt nervous, even though he knew he had nothing to hide.

"I…there was this magazine. I don't even remember which one now. But it said you were seen at a hotel in Bang-

kok, answering the door wrapped in a towel. There were…
two Thai girls at your door…"

"What? That's absurd."

"I know, I thought it had to be fake, but still, there was
a photo and it just looked so real, I had to ask…"

"Oh my god," Eli's face drained.

"What?"

"That did happen."

"What?"

"No, no, it's not like that. I haven't even thought about
it since. I had just gotten out of the shower getting ready
for my gig, and these two young Thai girls knocked on my
door, saying they were my massage therapists. But I didn't
order a massage. I told them they had the wrong guest, and
they left. I swear. It was really weird."

Angelina paused and looked deeply into his eyes. She
wanted to believe him. She held his gaze. She did believe
him. *Wait a minute.*

"Those girls…how young would you say they were?"

"Oh, I don't know. The youngest looked about twelve.
She was wearing makeup and high heels to make her look
older, but it didn't really help. Too young to be a massage
therapist, if you ask me."

"Eli…"

"Yes?"

"I think those girls might have been escorts. You know,
child prostitutes."

"Really?"

"What hotel were you staying at?"

"I don't know, it was fancy. The Grand Palace or something like that."

"I think we should look into it."

Petra Nicoll

"Shit. Yeah, if you think that's what it was."

"Let's try to do it anonymously. Exposing something as big as that could get both of us into deep trouble."

"Okay, I agree. But, Angelina?"

"Yes?"

"Let's wait until after Christmas. I mean, we could be wrong about it all—or we could be right and get swept up into something messy. I want to just enjoy this time with you and with my family."

Angelina hesitated before replying, "Okay. But first thing after Christmas, okay?"

"Absolutely." Eli pulled her close against him. "Do you know what?"

"What?"

"You are *hot,*" Eli lifted her up and swung her around the room as she giggled.

CHAPTER TWO

---∞∞∞---

AN UNEXPECTED VISITOR

This would be the first Christmas Eli would spend at the farm in Brownsville since he'd left at the age of seventeen. His parents, Robert and Carol, were ecstatic. None of them celebrated the holiday in the religious sense, but it still meant a lot to his parents that the family be together. Every year it had gotten harder and harder for them to hear friends talking about their holiday plans while their own son was thousands of miles away.

The holiday itself didn't hold much meaning to Eli, but this year he felt unusually nostalgic. He was eager to introduce Angelina to not only his parents and grandparents—Carol's mother and father were joining them from Coeur d'Alene, Idaho—but the farm where he grew up. He felt certain she would fall in love with all the animals and open space, just as he had as a child.

Eli and Angelina flew into Portland, Oregon and made the drive down in a rented Subaru Outback. He hoped to fit in as much as possible. He would undoubtedly be recognized by locals in town, but the more he could manage encounters with strangers along the way, the better. He wanted to feel "normal" during this trip.

Winter made it easier. Donning a wool hat, wide scarf, and bulky jacket, his most notable features were concealed.

"What do you think? Do I look like Eli Evans?"

"You look like a dork," Angelina teased from the passenger seat.

"Hey!" Eli pretended to look hurt. "You should be worried about being recognized yourself, miss award-winning actress."

"People outside of Hollywood don't know who I am yet," Angelina replied. "My movies have been more obscure."

"That's all about to change, once your screenplay gets swept up."

"I hope so. I haven't heard anything back from my agent yet."

"You will soon," Eli reached over and squeezed her hand.

It was dark by the time the two pulled into the long gravel road leading to the farmhouse in the early evening. There wasn't much of the land Angelina was able to see, but the stars had already captivated her as they stood outside the car.

"Look, Eli! You can actually see the whole sky from here! There's the Big Dipper!"

Eli wrapped his arms around her from behind and kissed her cheek. "It may be pretty, but I have the best view right here," he moved his lips to her eyelids, planting a kiss on each one.

"Are you ready to come in? This is your last chance to turn back," Eli teased.

"Why would I want to turn back? Let's go!"

Just then, the door flew open and Eli's mother came rushing out to greet them, not even wearing a coat.

"Ah! Angelina, welcome!" Eli smiled as he watched his mother throw her arms around his love.

"It's so nice to finally meet you!" Angelina smiled warmly.

"The pleasure is mine," the two stood holding each other's hands.

"Uhh, Mom? What about me?" Eli grinned.

As if noticing him for the first time, Carol walked over to Eli and wrapped her arms around his neck. "My son!" Eli leaned over as his mom kissed his forehead. "I am so glad you're here."

"Come in, everybody! You're letting a draft in!" Eli's father called out, pretending to be annoyed. He extended his hand toward Eli and pulled him toward his body for a heartfelt embrace, then gave Angelina a hug and a kiss on the cheek and escorted her into the house as Carol and Eli followed, arms linked.

Once inside, the sweet sounds and smells of home filled Eli's senses. A fire burned in the living room, where his parents were already roasting chestnuts. A Christmas tree was in the same corner as always—adorned with ornaments he recognized he'd made as a child that he'd all but forgotten about.

Robert caught Angelina's gaze. "Come, come," he gestured for her to follow him to the tree. "Did you see this one?" He pointed to an ornament that framed a picture of Eli when he was eight years old, with buck teeth and a cowlick. "Handsome devil, isn't he?" Robert chuckled.

"The most handsome ever," Angelina winked back at him.

"Eli! Come here, boy. Let me get a good look at you!" Eli's grandmother entered from the kitchen, where she'd been preparing her infamous holiday fudge.

"Oma," Eli kissed her cheek—he'd always used the German words for grandmother and grandfather to address his mother's parents. "So nice to see you!"

"My, how you've grown. It has been too long since you visited last, but your Opa and I sure are proud of you."

"Thanks, Oma. Where is Opa?"

"He's in his favorite room," Eli's grandmother smiled mischievously as the toilet flushed.

"Must you all embarrass me in front of Angelina already?" Eli laughed.

"She might as well learn what it's really like in the Evans family, don't you think? My dear, welcome," his grandmother turned to Angelina. "We do hope you'll make yourself at home here from the start."

"Certainly, thank you," Angelina held his grandmother's hand between both of hers. "It's a pleasure to meet you."

The family continued their introductions and words of welcome amid a flurry of activity—Carol was bringing out glasses of fruit punch as Robert filled a bowl of chestnuts and placed it on the dining room table. The table was already set for dinner—a feast of various cheeses, crackers, a Waldorf salad, roasted carrots and potatoes, corn casserole, and a mushroom risotto.

"Come back in the summer, Angelina, and the meal will come entirely from our garden," Carol shared. "Only the cheese and the nuts are from our land, but everything is organic and vegetarian—Eli has shared how that's important to you, as it is to us."

"I'm sure everything will be delicious," Angelina smiled.

She was so used having to explain her reasons for being vegetarian, that it was a welcome relief to simply be understood.

ELI AND ANGELINA had a week to spend at the Brownsville farm. They would head back to California on December 30th to ring in the New Year together in their new home before each of them had to continue working. Eli's tour picked up again January 3rd, although he hadn't even looked at the schedule yet. He wanted to immerse himself in his time off.

Carol and Robert delighted in showing Angelina their property. The 2,000-square-foot 1940s farmhouse had been lovingly restored with their own hands. Four hundred acres of national forest ran up against their thirty-acre property, offering a stunning view from every direction.

The next morning, Eli eagerly showed Angelina the creek that ran through the back of the property.

"This is where I spent countless hours as a child," he shared. "I wrote my first song while sitting on that rock over there."

"It's beautiful, Eli," Angelina replied. "It reminds me of where I grew up, at the ashram."

"Am I able to visit there?" Eli was curious about her past.

"I don't know. Someday. I mean, my parents are still there, so yes probably someday," Angelina became quiet. "Those weren't the best years of my life though, you know. At least not as I got older."

"I know," Eli kissed the top of her head. "When you're ready."

Eli became quiet himself. "Angelina?" he spoke in a serious voice.

"Yes?"

"There's something very important I have to ask you."

Angelina began to feel somewhat uncomfortable. "Go ahead."

"Have you ever milked a cow?"

Angelina burst out laughing. "You are rotten!" She gently punched his arm. "Are you serious? No, I have never milked a cow."

"Well, you're about to," Eli swept her up off her feet and carried her to the barn.

Although squeamish at first, Eli coached Angelina through her first milking experience, and she managed to fill half a bucket.

"You know, there's a hayloft up there," Eli gestured above. "In case, maybe, you feel like milking something else," he winked.

"That's so romantic, Eli," Angelina laughed sarcastically.

"Kidding aside, have you ever made love in a hayloft? You're missing out, I swear."

"No, I have not. You have?" she nudged him.

"Actually, I haven't either," Eli admitted with a smile. "But I always wanted to. With the right girl."

"Okay," Angelina grinned. "Let's do it."

Eli took her hand and led her up the ladder. Both were oblivious to the sounds and smells of cows down below as they playfully and passionately let themselves go.

ELI FELT LIKE a young boy on Christmas morning. Although he had enough wealth to buy himself the most lavish gifts he'd ever desired, the preciousness and thoughtfulness of the gifts he received from his parents meant more to him than anything else. Most items they'd made themselves—such as a wool scarf from his mother and wooden fountain pen his father had turned in his wood shop. They'd also bought Angelina a beautiful necklace, which Eli loved placing around her neck. He had a gift for her too, but he wanted to give it to her later in private.

Eli had brought gifts for every member of his family, as well—jewelry for his mother and grandmother and new pocket watches for his father and grandfather. His choices lacked creativity, but he never was good at knowing what to buy for his family. They always insisted they had everything they needed, and anything more would be frivolous. Nonetheless, they received his gifts graciously.

"Wait," his mother interjected as Angelina and Eli were about to get up and move to the kitchen. "There's one more gift."

"For whom?" Eli asked.

"The person who earns it," his mother winked.

"Ah! I almost forgot," Eli smiled. "The pickle ornament!"

"The what?" Angelina asked, confused.

"The pickle ornament. It's a German tradition," Eli explained. "There's a glass pickle hidden somewhere on the tree. Whoever finds it first receives a small gift."

"Fun!" she exclaimed.

"It's just for the kids," Eli's mother added.

"That means us," Eli clarified to Angelina with a chuckle.

The two set about searching the tree for the hidden ornament. In the end, Angelina came up with it. "Aha! This must be it!" she exclaimed.

"Yep, you found the pickle. This is for you," Carol pulled out a wooden box from underneath her chair.

The box was hand carved and engraved, "From Brownsville, with Love." The image of a home with a heart inside of it was framed by the shape of the state of Oregon.

"Every time you look at it, we want you to remember that you always have a home here with us," Carol smiled. "Both of you."

"Thank you," Angelina's eyes welled up with tears as she hugged Carol first, and then Robert.

Eli didn't like to get emotional in front of his parents, but it meant so much to him that they saw in Angelina what he saw in her. Pure love.

THE FAMILY'S WEEK together went all too fast, despite the long days. All of them stayed up late each night, sharing family stories and playing music. It was refreshing for Eli to not have to play any of his "hits," and to not be the star of the show. His grandparents chose just to listen, but Eli and his parents took turns playing guitar and singing lead vocals. Angelina insisted on singing harmony only, until the final night.

"Please, Angelina?" Eli had insisted. "This is our last night together. My parents would love to hear you sing. You have a beautiful voice, don't be shy."

"No, no. Truly, I love listening to you all."

"I have something that might change your mind," Eli grinned. "I was going to wait for a private moment to give it to you, but I'm running out of time and I think now is actually the perfect moment. Wait here." Eli went out to the car and returned with a large, wrapped box.

"I had this shipped to Brownville from India. I picked it up at the post office the other day—when I said I was going to get bread," Eli winked.

Angelina was surprised she hadn't picked up on him being up to something.

"Careful, it's fragile," he placed the box before her.

Angelina delicately unwrapped the package. "Oh, Eli! It's beautiful!" An antique BINA harmonium sat before her.

"I asked for the best. And I thought you'd like one with a history."

"Oh, I do. I love it!" Angelina held Eli in a long embrace. "Thank you. You didn't have to do that."

"I wanted to. But…" Eli grinned. "Now you have to play something for us. Go on. Sing for us."

She didn't need much coaxing this time. Angelina couldn't wait to get her fingers on that gorgeous instrument.

"I already tuned it," Eli smiled.

"I…I'll play something new I've been working on," Angelina said shyly. She began to play but quickly stopped.

"What's wrong?" Eli asked.

"It's just…it's not tuned correctly."

Eli's parents began to tease him.

"What do you mean? I know how to tune an instrument," Eli felt slightly defensive.

"Yes, but you tuned the 'A' note to a frequency of 440 hertz. I prefer to play in 432."

"Oh, okay. I figured you'd prefer standard concert pitch. I didn't even know you knew about playing in 432 hertz."

Angelina smiled back at him. "I do."

Eli was speechless. He'd underestimated her. He suddenly realized he'd placed himself on a pedestal in their relationship, at least in terms of musical knowledge.

Angelina asked for the tuner and changed the harmonium to the pitch she liked. "There," she said proudly and began to play again.

It wasn't only Eli who was swept away by her music and her voice. His family was equally in awe. *Why didn't I notice this before?* he wondered. Her pitch matched that of some of the new material he'd been creating and performing. *Incredible.*

Later that night, after the two had gone to bed, Eli could not fall asleep. He couldn't stop thinking about Angelina's performance earlier in the night. He knew intuitively that something had changed inside of him—he felt for the first time what his audience members felt when he played his new material. *Who knew Angelina's music could do that to me, too.*

What does this mean? he questioned. If he was ever going to fall asleep, he needed to jolt himself out of all this thinking. Not wanting to wake Angelina, he slowly crept outside of their bed and went to the bathroom down the hall. He splashed cold water on his face and looked up into the mirror.

"Ah!" he exclaimed.

"Gotcha!" Michael's face protruded out from the mirror before he shape-shifted into the full human form Eli recognized.

"Jesus Christ, Michael, are you trying to scare me half to death? And my family?"

"I was only having a little fun. Relax," Michael chuckled. "They're all fast asleep."

"Alright, well what are you doing here anyway?"

"You act like you're disappointed to see me."

"I'm not. Well, I am. I don't know. It's the middle of the night. I'm with my family. What is so important?"

"Did you or did you not ask me to keep you on your path?"

"I…I did. What have I done?"

"It's nothing you've done, it's what you need to do

next, Eli. You've been enjoying yourself this past couple of months. That's good, that's great. I'm very happy for you. Spending time with family and with Angelina is important. But I'm here to help you with the work that lies ahead. The work that this planet desperately needs right now. There isn't much time..."

"What do you mean? What else is there? I mean, I'm still supporting all my charities, creating entrepreneurship opportunities for women in third-world countries, sponsoring sustainable initiatives...I haven't exactly been sitting on my ass, you know."

"That work you have been doing is great, I admit. But there's more to your purpose here on this planet, remember? What did we talk about, with your music?"

"With the new material? I'm still experimenting with it. People are digging it."

"True, true. But, what did you realize tonight? When Angelina played?"

"Well...I've been trying to figure that out myself. She played in 432 hertz."

"I know."

"I didn't know she knew about that."

"She does."

"Yeah, I know that now. But what does that mean?"

"It means, Eli, that you have an opportunity before you, and so does she. The vibration of society needs to be raised. Big time, these days. You need to carry on the great work of John Lennon, Bob Marley, Carlos Santana, and more.

"Nearly all music today is played in 440 hertz, creating subtle disharmony in its listeners, and resulting in anxiety and illness. You understand this, and so does Angelina. Playing in 432 hertz, with respect to Earth's natural vibration, resonates with the heart chakra. It repairs DNA and restores both spiritual and mental health. It reminds people of who they really are, Eli. Remember?"

"I do. I mean, nearly all of my new music is in 432. You know this."

"It is, but it's not reaching enough people. I was thinking, have you ever noticed how everyone in your band is male?"

"Ha! Yeah, our tour bus has always been one big sausage factory."

"There is an opportunity for your music to reach even more people by incorporating a female voice. A woman's touch, if you will."

"Wait, you want Angelina to go on tour with me?"

"If the shoe fits…"

"But, wait. We just moved in together. Isn't that a bit… much?"

"What are you worried about, Eli?"

"Shit, I mean, talk about a test of our relationship…"

"Is that such a bad thing? There is a lot to be learned through relationship, Eli. Far more than one can ever learn single."

"But what about her acting? She's busy enough with auditions and writing screenplays as it is."

"Well, it is up to her of course, but it is possible for her to manage both careers. She need not play on every track of your album or perform at every show."

"Okay. True. I'd need to talk to her about all this."

Michael smiled. "Yes, please do. Oh, and Eli? One more thing…remember to ask her about what you'd promised to do after Christmas. That will be all, ta-ta!" Michael disappeared back into the mirror.

Holy shit. Eli thought to himself as he finally crawled back into bed. *This is too much to process right now. I'll think about it tomorrow.*

"Who were you talking to?" Angelina turned over and asked sleepily. "Is everything okay?"

"Hmm? Oh, yeah. No one, just…my dad. Go back to sleep, Ang. I love you," Eli planted a kiss on her forehead before rolling over and falling fast asleep.

CHAPTER THREE

DISRUPTING THE SYSTEM

Eli mulled over what had happened with Michael that last night at his parents' home throughout the duration of his and Angelina's flight back to Los Angeles. He was noticeably distracted.

"Is everything okay?" Angelina asked while seated next to him on the flight.

"Hmm?" he tried to buy time. He wanted to tell her about the conversation he'd had with Michael, but he still wasn't sure of the best way to go about it. Thus far, he hadn't told Angelina details of his relationship with his guide, or the fact that Michael would manifest physically before him.

"It seems like something is bothering you. What did you talk about with your dad last night? You've been acting weird ever since."

"Have I?" There were a number of reasons Eli's head wouldn't settle. He wasn't sure he wanted Angelina to go on tour with him. Would she be able to handle seeing what it was like? He wasn't sure their relationship could withstand it. And he didn't want to distract her from her developing acting career.

Another topic bothering him was what he'd promised he'd look into after Christmas. Was the hotel in Bangkok operating a sex trafficking ring? *I can talk about that now, instead of the tour,* he realized.

"Well, there is something bothering me. Remember how we talked about looking into that Bangkok hotel?"

"Yes, I do remember."

"I'll need to make a call about that when we get back. I'm kind of dreading what we find out."

"I understand."

After Eli and Angelina settled back into their home and celebrated a quiet New Years together, Eli held his promise. He called the National Human Trafficking Hotline on January 2nd, and reported what he'd seen. He asked to remain anonymous, though he suspected a leak would happen somewhere along the line. The media was ruthless, even in regard to sensitive information.

He remained distracted throughout the rest of that day and night. His tour would resume the following day, with a gig in San Francisco. Angelina was going to come with him since her acting commitments didn't begin until a couple of days later and she had friends she wanted to visit in the city before the show.

Her presence at his show took on new meaning for him. *What if I brought her up on stage?* he wondered. *Perhaps then we could both see the impact she might have on the audience.* Without her knowledge, he packed her harmonium, just in case.

ELI WAS EQUAL parts excited and anxious as he prepared to go back out on stage for the first time in two months. He missed the adrenaline rush, but he was nervous about how Angelina might react to his bringing her out on stage. He had avoided asking her in advance because he feared she might deny the opportunity outright.

As he stood at the side of the stage before the main set, he could see her in the front row, off to the left. He winked at her, and she winked back. The band had already walked out and begun to take their places at their respective instruments. The crowd was cheering like crazy. *Only two months off and I'd nearly forgotten what a high this is*, he thought.

"Eli! Eli! Eli!" the audience chanted.

He walked out to center stage and lowered the microphone just a tad. He slowly struck the first few chords of his latest release, a song titled "Take Me to the Mountain," which quieted the audience. As the drummer and bass player kicked in and the energy of the song elevated, the audience again erupted. When he began to sing, he could already see members of the front row getting goosebumps. Some were moved to tears.

Damn, this feels good, he thought. By the third song, his courage was elevated to the point where he made eye contact with Angelina.

"And now, I'd like to introduce you all to a very special guest," he grinned. He could see a bit of color drain from Angelina's face, but he continued. "If you like my new sound, you'll love what this incredible woman has to offer," he signaled to a crew member to bring out the harmonium. "Angelina, will you play us a song?"

She was about to shake her head no, but the audience had already welcomed her with open arms. Their cheers escalated to the point where she felt she had no choice. She gave Eli a death glare but smiled despite her anxiety and made her way to the stage.

Angelina awkwardly approached the stage, not sure of where to go. Eli placed a kiss on her cheek and his palm on the small of her back, guiding her to sit on the cushion laid out before the harmonium. A member of the crew adjusted a microphone before it.

"What am I supposed to play?!" Angelina whispered in Eli's ear.

"How about the song you played for my parents? That was beautiful."

"Okay," she replied, reluctantly.

Angelina took a seat on the cushion and a few deep breaths before hitting the first few notes on the harmonium. By the time her voice entered to accompany the melody, the audience was captivated. She touched their hearts in the way only a female voice could—accompanied by the right instrument in the right tone. Eli stood by and witnessed the crowd's reaction. *Something big is happening*, he thought.

He was aware of a similar reaction when he played, but he saw the potential for a harmonic relationship that amplified what he was able to produce. *Is Angelina seeing this?!* he wondered. He wasn't sure, as she sang with her eyes closed. He looked out again at the audience. Every member stood completely still and silent. *Their souls are deep in this moment*, Eli could feel it.

As Angelina finished the final note of the song, he saw her open her eyes. For a while, the audience didn't react at all. Angelina entered back into the world before her and felt her earlier anxiety return. *Didn't they like it?* she wondered. Tears ran down people's faces—but Eli recognized them as tears of joy. He smiled.

One person in the front row began to clap. The sound

seemed to awaken the rest of the room, as each member joined in, adding whistles and cheers that brought each of them back from wherever it was they had been. Angelina smiled as tears ran down her own cheek. She looked over at Eli.

I told you, he mouthed.

Angelina shyly made her way down from the stage as Eli approached the microphone.

"I believe we'll be hearing more from this beautiful woman in the future, don't you think? Give it up for Angelina!" Eli asked the audience as they cheered loudly and screamed in unison: "Angelina…Angelina…Angelina!"

ELI EXPECTED AS enthusiastic of a reaction from Angelina after the show. What he received instead surprised him.

"Love! How did it feel?!" he reached out to her warmly but was met with a cold stare.

"How it felt isn't what I want to address right now," she answered.

"What do you mean?"

"That wasn't right of you to put me on the spot like that, Eli. You planned that. You brought my harmonium, and you didn't even tell me."

Eli tried to cover his sheepish look with optimism. "But you were a hit! If I had asked you, you would have said no."

"Actually, I probably would have said yes. But you made that decision for me."

"Well, it's over now. I'm sorry I didn't ask you, I didn't know you'd be upset."

"You have to communicate better with me Eli. Sometimes I think you're hiding a lot from me…important things. Things that are even more important than this. This experience proved my instincts were right."

"But you have to admit, it felt great out there, didn't it? Did you see the audience's reaction? You really touched them."

"I didn't see it. I felt it afterward. But please don't change the subject. If we are going to build a relationship together, we have to be honest. That should be the foundation we build upon."

Angelina could sense Eli's discomfort. He had a tendency to want to walk away when conflict arose. His gaze was moving toward the catering table in the back of the room.

"Stay with me, love," she precipitated. "We have to turn toward each other when things get tough, not away."

Eli met her eyes. "Okay, I hear you. I said I'm sorry."

"I forgive you," Angelina stood tall and kissed him. "Can you tell me why you didn't ask me in advance, though? I sense there's something else."

Eli fidgeted with a button on his jacket. "I…I actually wasn't sure I was going to invite you on stage. I wanted to see how it felt in the moment. I…I'm actually afraid of what it might mean for our relationship. And your career. And my career, for that matter."

"Nothing has changed, Eli."

"But it could. You saw them out there. They loved you. They were moved to tears by your music. Mich—I mean, I think there's an opportunity for us to have an even greater impact on the world if we work together. And that scares me," Eli felt released after admitting the truth.

Angelina was silent, allowing Eli to continue. "Would you…want to perform with me? You don't have to go to every show. But would you want to come to some? Perhaps have a track or two on my next album? What do you say?"

"I'd have to think about it. I'd have auditions to work around, and film shoots. And I'm still hoping someone buys my screenplay…"

"I know. Think about it all you want. Take your time."

"What do you think about it? Is that what you really want?"

"I think so…"

"You'll have to do better than that," Angelina laughed.

"I do want it, but like I said it scares me."

"Sometimes…when something scares us, that means we have to do it. I experienced that tonight. You scared the shit out of me calling me up onstage unexpected like that, Eli," Angelina punched him in the arm playfully.

"And you played beautifully," he bent down and kissed her tenderly.

"Okay, Eli Evans. I don't need to think about it. I feel it. Let's do this," Angelina stood boldly.

"Really?" Eli was surprised at how excited he felt.

"Really."

Eli and Angelina flew home together late that night. She would have to attend a meeting with her agent early the next day, so she went to bed immediately upon their arrival. But Eli stayed awake, rummaging through some of the boxes he had yet to unpack.

He was listening to music through his headphones when he felt a tap on his shoulder. He turned around, expecting to see Angelina.

"Michael!" he exclaimed, pulling off his headphones.

"Shh…" Michael brought his finger to his lips. "Angelina is sleeping."

"What are you doing here?"

"When are you going to stop asking me that question? You know the reason why I always come…"

"You said you come when I'm straying from my path. But I've done everything we talked about last time."

"True, you have. You made an important phone call. And you brought Angelina into your music. Although you should have talked to Angelina about playing with you first."

"Oh god, I don't need you to lecture me on that, too," Eli rolled his eyes.

"Don't worry, Angelina did that job for me. She's one of your guides too, you know…" Michael paused for him to take that message in.

"She is a good teacher," Eli agreed.

"She's even better than you realize, Eli. But that is not why I've come."

"Okay, so why are you here?"

"It seems you are newly committed to your role as a messenger and healer through your music, and now you will do so with added collaboration with Angelina, so that is very good. But in order to make the impact you are here to make, you must understand the bigger picture. You must see what is truly going on in the world. Beneath the surface, there is a scheme being orchestrated by the extremely wealthy."

"Umm…doesn't that category include me at this point?" Eli's tone lacked humility, which Michael noted.

"Your wealth is pocket change compared to what members of this elite group have control over. But that must change in this lifetime of yours."

"You've kind of lost me, Michael."

"You have the potential—and the karmic responsibility—of disrupting a long-held chain of power controlled by the central banking system. This banking system, through its practices, covertly dictates which countries and which communities live luxuriously, and likewise those that live in poverty."

"How does it do that?"

"In a nutshell, by creating money out of nothing, charging interest on it and devaluating the purchasing power of the dollar and other monetary units. This system has created an exploited society reliant on debt, forcing people to work jobs that drain their life force.

"The majority of people have become slaves to money—or rather, to their debt—which means they have to rely on the establishment to save them through more loans, credit cards, and fees. In other words, the rich are getting richer while the poor are getting poorer."

"So how can I—or anyone—make a dent in that system?"

"People already are. There are highly evolved humans who are changing the world banking system and equalizing countries, communities, and individuals through cryptocurrencies."

"Cryptocurrencies…you mean like Bitcoin?"

"Yes, Bitcoin, Litecoin, Ethereum…there are numerous."

Eli scratched his head. "That reminds me…when I was home over Christmas, I ran into an old friend of mine, Dwayne, at the post office. Well, he wasn't a close friend or anything, I mean he was kind of the geek in school. He said something to me I didn't understand."

"Yes?" Michael smiled.

"He said, 'Yo Eli, can you believe how much that crypto account I set up for you is worth?' He went on to say I must not need it anyway since I'm 'rolling in dough' from my music. I was in a hurry, so I didn't stop to talk to him, but I saw him drive away in a Ferrari, which is seriously shocking for Brownsville, Oregon."

"He was one of your messengers too, Eli. He was there to remind you of something. By the way, that answers your question."

"What question?"

"The one you keep asking me—'why are you here?'"

"I don't get it."

"Sometimes, Eli, you can be so dense."

"Hey!"

"Okay, I didn't mean that. But seriously, you need everything spelled out for you directly. I'm just going to give you another clue."

"What is it?"

"Check your safe," Michael nodded in the direction of a heavy, fireproof safe in the corner of the room that he hadn't opened in years. He hadn't yet found a place for it since they'd moved in.

"Okay…"

"Goodnight!" Michael left in a flash, as usual.

CHAPTER FOUR

———— ∞∞∞ ————

THE PHONE CALL

Why does he always leave me like that? Eli shook his head at Michael's tendency to leave just as unannounced as he'd arrive. Per Michael's suggestion, Eli headed over to the safe he hadn't opened in years. His father had bought it for him when he first left their home in Brownsville, as a means to keep his first record contract safe. *A heck of a lot of good that contract did me*, he thought with disdain, remembering how his first label and manager had taken advantage of him. He acknowledged, however, that it did play a part in leading him to the enormously successful position he was in today.

Eli made a lucky guess as to the combination of the lock to the safe; it was one he had used often during his high school years. He blew on a stack of papers inside, forgetting that the fan would blow the dust back in his face. Coughing slightly, he pulled the papers out.

On top was a welcome letter from his first record label. At the beginning of his career, he had saved every document he'd received; he thought it would be neat to give them to his grandchildren someday. At the time, he had no idea just how far his career would take him and how famous he'd become.

Beneath the papers from his record label was a stack of his first fan letters. *I completely forgot about these*, he thought. Now, all of his fan mail was filtered through his publicist and only a select few were shared with him. He remembered how much those first letters had meant to him but also how strange it had felt to receive them.

Next, he found copies of his birth certificate and old medical records. His very first passport rested at the bottom of the safe. He flipped through it, amazed at how it had gone from zero stamps to full within the first two years after he started touring. Eli felt a wave of gratitude for all that he'd been able to experience in his young life.

His memories were pulled back to the present as he re-membered why he had opened the safe in the first place. *What the heck did Michael want me to find?* he thought. He gathered all the documents around him to toss back into the safe. But just then, a small piece of paper fell from the stack.

"Eli – here's your private key. DON'T LOSE THIS!!! – Dwayne" was scrawled in messy handwriting, followed by a series of codes. Suddenly, he remembered what the guy he'd run into at the Brownsville post office over Christmas was referring to. *Bitcoin,* he thought.

Dwayne had convinced him to invest in the cryptocur-rency when he was in high school, probably around 2010. He didn't understand it then—and he still didn't now—but Dwayne had insisted Bitcoin was "the next big thing" and offered to set everything up for him. He'd made a measly investment of $100—tips from a couple of his shows at a Eugene coffeehouse—and never gave it another thought.

How do I even access that account? Eli wondered. He became obsessed with understanding what Michael had so deeply wanted him to remember. It was past 1 a.m., but Eli pulled out his laptop and began to research cryptocurrencies. He had never paid much attention to his finances before—his accountant took care of all that. *Perhaps I should have gotten more involved,* he thought now.

He read about the difference between "fiat money" and cryptocurrency. He had never thought about what was really behind the dollar before—that on its own, it has no intrinsic value. When the dollar was taken off the gold standard in 1971 (currency that has uses other than as a medium of exchange, often created from gold or silver), the only value left was what the government assigned its value to be through the Federal Reserve. *Fiat money has nothing to back it but debt,* he realized.

Cryptocurrencies began to take off with Bitcoin in 2009, which was created by an anonymous programmer who described the currency as a "peer-to-peer electronic cash system," Eli read. The system is completely decentralized, so there are no servers and no central controlling authority—cryptocurrencies are not backed by the government, or the Federal Reserve.

A public ledger of all transactions used by every participant within the network—a system called the Blockchain—is available to everyone, which means it operates on the principle of transparency. The process is ensured with strong cryptography, hence the name. Eli learned that cryptocurrencies are stored in "wallets" offered by major exchanges, or they can be stored in off-line wallets. Either way, the currency only exists in the ether.

He looked back down at the series of details on Dwayne's

note. He'd listed the name of the wallet, password, and other identifying factors needed in order to access his Bitcoin account. He set about downloading the necessary software onto his computer. It felt like forever before he was finally able to enter into his account. When he did, he thought there must be some mistake.

That $100 he'd invested in 2010 was now worth...*over sixty million dollars*?! He couldn't believe what he was seeing. *Can this be right?!* Eli went about googling what was going on in the industry and came across similar stories of people who had long ago invested minuscule amounts of money that had now turned into fortunes. It felt surreal. The amount of money wasn't shocking to him in itself—he had earned that amount of money throughout his career—but this was money he hadn't had to *earn*. It was simply there.

He became increasingly interested in learning how to invest more—and not only invest but to "mine" for Bitcoins, something he had read about in that night's hours of research. Bitcoin mining was the means through which new Bitcoin were released, which could be solved through computationally difficult puzzles. *I've always been good at math*, he realized with a smile.

It was not over Eli's head that he was already extremely wealthy. Nevertheless, he was driven by what would be possible to accomplish in the world with massive amounts of additional abundance. The philanthropic projects he'd been initiating seemed like small fry, compared to what he now realized was possible for him to achieve—with the help of the right people. No dream was too big. Heck, he could rebuild cities, or third-world *countries*, with access to the kind of capital he felt cryptocurrencies could open up to him.

Eli was so ramped up he knew he wouldn't be able to

sleep that night. In any case, he placed all of the documents he'd removed back in the safe and re-locked it. He laid down on the couch to try to at least get some rest—he knew if he joined Angelina in bed, his tossing and turning would keep her up. After 5 a.m., he was finally able to fall asleep.

WHEN ELI AWOKE after 10 a.m. the next day, Angelina had already left for her meeting. *I made you some juice in the fridge. See you tonight. XOXO* she'd written in the note she'd left on the island in their expansive kitchen. He had band rehearsal that afternoon, but the two had made plans to meet at home for a late dinner.

He didn't usually read the newspaper, but that morning he collected the stack of newspapers his security guard had left for him at the front door to read with his breakfast. He was curious if there were any articles on cryptocurrencies. He settled onto a bar stool and laid one of the papers out before him, sipping his breakfast juice. The headlines always seemed the same—another mass school shooting, protests on gun violence against African Americans, corruption in the White House, Puerto Rico still lacking electricity and infrastructure after the storm. *Now I remember why I stopped reading the paper*, he thought. *It's so damn depressing.*

He threw the paper aside and made another unusual decision to reach for an entertainment gossip newspaper that everyone knew not to take seriously. *I need to read about something meaningless after all that*, he thought. He casually opened the paper, but the first headline he saw caused his mouth to drop open. *Rock Star Eli Evans Exposes Elite Sex Trafficking Ring.*

His heart raced as his eyes scrolled through the article. The writer claimed Eli had been overheard reporting a possible sex scandal in a Bangkok hotel, and that further investigation had revealed a massive ring operating out of…*Los Angeles*?! He had no idea if the article was true—it was in the Entertainment section, after all—but who in the hell "overheard" him report the incident in Bangkok?! He'd made the call from his landline phone at home…the same home he was in now. *Is my phone line tapped? He wondered. Are there hidden cameras here? What the fuck?!*

The property was surrounded by a tall, locked gate and 24-hour security guards and surveillance. *How could anyone have managed to get past all that?!* Eli's state bordered on panic. He paced back and forth in the living room, paranoid he was being watched through the tall windows. *I need to get to the bottom of this*, he thought. He slipped on some shoes and walked outside to the front gate.

"Good morning, Eli," Jake, his lead security guard waved.

"Good morning, Jake. Say, you haven't seen any weird activity around here lately, have you? Any signs of someone having entered the property?"

"No, sir. We would have told you if we had."

"That's what I figured."

"Why do you ask?"

"It's just…" Eli considered sharing what he saw in the paper but then he realized someone who worked at the hotline—or otherwise got a hold of its records—may have recognized his voice and tipped off the paper.

"Never mind, it's nothing. Thanks, Jake."

Eli returned to his house, feeling somewhat relieved that the information could have leaked by means other than someone having been in his home. Nevertheless, he picked up his cell phone and called his bodyguard, who he usually only hired for public appearances, just to be sure.

"Hey, Ron. Listen, can you come around before noon today? There's something I want you to check."

"Absolutely. I'll come over right now."

"Thanks, I appreciate it."

When Ron arrived, Eli had showered and changed into comfortable rehearsal clothes. He explained his concern that his landline phone might be tapped and wanted him to check it out. Ron met him back in the living room an hour later, having completed a detailed analysis of the entire home. Nothing.

"Great, thanks, Ron. There's been nothing else weird going on, has there?" he added as an afterthought.

"Nothing more than the usual—you know, girls sending their panties in the mail, minor threats that turn out to be empty."

"Okay. Got it. Thanks for the peace of mind, bro."

"That's why you hired me. Later, man. See you tomorrow night at the Coliseum."

"Right, see you then," Eli hadn't given much thought to his show the next day, held locally in Los Angeles. He glanced at his watch. He'd better leave for rehearsal. *I'm probably blowing that article out of proportion*, he thought. He picked up the stack of newspapers and magazines and tossed them into the recycling bin before grabbing his keys and heading to his car.

ANGELINA GOT HOME around 7 p.m. that night before Eli had arrived. She'd given their chef the night off, so as to surprise Eli with a traditional Indian meal. She had big news to share, and she wanted to make the night extra special.

He came through the door shortly after 8 p.m. to the

aroma of chickpea curry, fried vegetable samosas, garlic naan bread, and chai. "Ta-da!" Angelina smiled with pride. "Perfect timing!"

Eli met her hug and kissed the top of her head. "It smells great, love." His response was genuine but not as enthusiastic as Angelina had expected.

"What's wrong? Is everything okay?" she asked.

"Yeah, yeah. It's been a long day, that's all."

"Well take a load off, babe. I've got cooking and cleanup tonight. Go on, have a seat at the table before it gets cold," she winked.

Eli followed her suggestion and took in the bounty before them. It did look fantastic. He wished he weren't so distracted by everything on his mind...Michael's visit and the Bitcoin discovery the night before, the article in the paper that morning, and a band rehearsal that hadn't gone all that well. Still, he appreciated Angelina's efforts.

"This looks great, Angelina. Thank you."

"You're very welcome," she smiled. "I wanted to do something special tonight. I have some big news."

For a moment, Eli experienced a mixture of excitement and fear. "Wait, are you pregnant?" his eyes widened.

Angelina laughed. "No, no. It's not that."

"What is it?"

"Well, you know how I had a meeting with my agent this morning?"

"Yes..."

"You know my screenplay that was optioned last spring?"

"Yes..."

"It's been SOLD! Revolution Studios is going all in!"

"What? Congratulations!" Eli kicked back his chair and grabbed Angelina by the waist, swinging her around the room. "I knew you could do it!"

Angelina giggled. "Thank you. I haven't told you the best part yet though…"

"There's more?"

"Yes. Guess who's going to star in the film?"

"No way…you are?"

Angelina nodded.

"Hell yeah! That's my woman!" Eli grinned from ear to ear.

"Let the craziness begin…"

Eli suddenly remembered their discussion after the San Francisco concert. "Wait, are you still going to do music with me?"

"I don't know. I suppose so. I mean, I want to. But I'm also about to get really busy…"

"True. I really hope you can do this with me though… you saw how the crowd was the other night."

"I know. I will try my best to do both, I promise."

"You know, my show tomorrow night is here in Los Angeles…."

"Oh, is it?" Angelina rarely knew the specifics of Eli's tour.

"It is. Do you want to join me again? You can perform the same song as the other night?"

Angelina paused to consider the proposition. "I suppose I could…"

"Good. It's settled then," Eli winked.

"But for now, eat your dinner! It's getting cold," Angelina smiled.

Eli forgot all about what had been bothering him earlier during the day and night as he dug into the delicious meal before him. He was so proud of his girl.

THE FOLLOWING NIGHT was a replay of the night in San Francisco—excluding Angelina's initial reluctance to go on stage. She felt more confident and eager to share her voice with a larger audience—the Los Angeles Memorial Coliseum sat over 90,000 people, and the show was sold out.

Once again, the crowd was moved to tears and prolonged silence by her voice and the sound and soul released through the harmonium. For a moment, Eli thought she might upstage him. His fans were loyal, however, and responded to his music with the usual enthusiasm and excitement and occasional pandemonium. At one point, he did steal a glance at his bodyguard off to the side of the stage, just to ensure all was well. He received a nod that relaxed him.

After the show, he embraced Angelina. "Well, what did you think this time?" he asked.

"I'm beginning to like it up there," Angelina winked.

"I told you so," Eli grinned. "It's becoming clear we'll need to record that song. The merchandise table is being inundated with requests for it."

"Okay. If you think it's a good idea, we can add it to your next album."

"I think it's a great idea."

The song, titled "Waterways," was recorded a few weeks later and included on Eli's album a few months after that. When he had a vision, he didn't waste any time manifesting it. He insisted on the song being the title track of the album, and since he called all the shots for his record label, that's what was done. Consumer response couldn't have been more optimistic; the song was downloaded over one million times its first day on the market.

Eli spared Angelina a lot of the typical promotion involved in the track and the album; she had become increasingly busy with her own acting career, and he didn't want to place more demands on her time than were necessary. She joined him for an occasional performance—especially ones that were local and involved charitable contributions—but he carried the bulk of the media interviews and gigs.

The times she was able to join him for a show were a special treat in more ways than one—despite having moved in together, their time together had become extremely limited over the last few months. Angelina's film was shot on location in Los Angeles, but her days were long—sometimes even overnight—and Eli was often out of the state and the country while on tour.

As the physical distance between them grew, the emotional distance did as well. Eli could feel himself getting further sidetracked from the things—and the people—most important to him. He hadn't seen his parents since Christmas, he saw Angelina a few days per month, at best, and his meditation and yoga practice had all but completely fallen by the wayside. He didn't yet realize it, but he grew more and more disconnected from himself and his purpose, on the verge of falling back into the depression he'd experienced earlier in his career, before meeting Michael.

To top it all off, he'd received reports from his publicist that the media was having a heyday with his relationship with Angelina. Ever since he'd invited her on stage, false rumors abounded that she had lip-synced, that he didn't compensate her for the track on his album, that she was only in a relationship with him because she was using his stardom to launch her own career...

Angelina largely ignored all of the accusations and reports, but Eli had a harder time disregarding them. He felt responsible for having brought Angelina into the drama that resulted from his fame. At no point did he have a harder time overlooking all of the unwanted attention that summer, than when he received a phone call on a rare day off at home.

"Hello?" he'd answered.

"Hello, Eli," a muffled voice replied.

"Who's calling?" Eli demanded, feeling immediately uncomfortable.

"No need to be hostile. I've called to warn you."

"Warn me about what?" Eli glanced vulnerably out the window toward his security guard.

"I can't say. Just stop doing what you're doing. They're onto you."

"Who's onto me? What am I doing?"

"Just be careful," the caller hung up without answering any of his questions. Eli's heart was pounding. He had no idea what to make of the call. He'd received nerve-wracking calls before, but never ones he had answered through his home phone line—they'd always come through his fan club number, or through his agent.

Immediately, he called his bodyguard. "Ron, I need you over here. ASAP."

"On my way."

Less than fifteen minutes later, Ron knocked on the door. Eli explained the unsettling call, and Ron went about trying to trace the source. Whoever had called had access to high-tech equipment, as the number was solidly blocked.

"I'll notify your security guards and put the property on high alert," he stated. "I'm spending the night here tonight," Ron left no room for negotiation. "Where's Angelina?"

"She's at the studio. She should be back late tonight."

"I'll call backup to meet her at the studio and escort her home."

Holy shit, Eli thought. *If my career has put her life in danger, I'll never forgive myself.*

Ron seemed to read his mind. "It's just a precaution. It's probably just some quack with expensive equipment."

"But, Eli?"

"Yes?"

"Can you think of anyone you may have upset? Who may have cause to do damage to your career?"

"I don't know. People talk shit about my career all the time. Anytime someone finds success, there are others trying to tear that person down."

"True, but those are usually people without money. Can you think of anyone with money that may have something against you? Someone in an elite crowd?"

The word "elite" triggered a memory. *That article on the sex trafficking ring.* He'd largely shrugged that issue aside, as it appeared to be brushed off as entertainment with no basis of truth by more reputable publications. He hadn't even told Angelina about it.

Maybe I should have. Shit. Maybe I also should have told Ron about it.

"Well, several months ago…I made an anonymous phone call to a sex trafficking hotline."

"You did what?"

"Yeah, when I was at a hotel in Bangkok before a show, these two young girls—I mean really young—mistakenly came to my door. They said they were my massage therapists. Angelina thought they might be part of a sex trafficking ring, so I reported it. I haven't heard anything about it since. Except…

"Yes?"

"There was an article in a gossip newspaper about it. It reported that I was 'overheard' reporting the incident. But I called from here—there was no one here except Angelina and I. Wait, you came that day. It's why I asked you to check the phone line for tapping."

"Shit, Eli, you should have told me all this."

"I can see that now, but I thought maybe I was overreacting. Also, someone from the hotline could have gotten a hold of the report. I didn't think it meant there had to have been someone in my home or listening to my calls."

"Eli, exposing a sex trafficking ring is a huge deal. Huge. No matter how or who found out about your role in that, when word gets to the ringleaders, you're likely to have a bounty on your head."

"Well thanks, that's reassuring."

"Don't worry, our team is on it. I'm calling in backup for your property tonight too. We'll be staying with you 24/7 until this is sorted out."

"Alright," Eli had no desire to argue.

An hour later, Angelina came through the door escorted by Eric, a bodyguard Eli recognized from previous gigs.

"Oh, thank God," Eli hugged her close.

"Eli, what is all this about?"

Ron interjected, "It's probably nothing, Angelina, we're just taking some extra precautions for a while."

"I got a strange phone call tonight. Somebody called to 'warn' me that I needed to 'stop doing what I'm doing,' and that 'they're onto me,' whoever 'they' are. The call was properly blocked."

"Jesus, Eli."

"I don't know what it's about, but I think it might have something to do with the sex trafficking ring—the one in Bangkok that I called about."

"Shit. I'm so sorry I made you call that in."

"You didn't make me do anything, I did what had to be done," Eli kissed her on the cheek. "The guys are staying here tonight. We'll be alright."

Angelina turned to Ron and Eric, "Thank you, guys."

"Just doing our job. We'll be on surveillance, but please, I know it's hard but try not to mind us. Try to relax tonight."

Eli turned to Angelina, "Babe, why don't you take a hot bath and try not to think about this?"

"Easier said than done."

"I know, I know. But just try. We're not going anywhere."

"Okay. Fair enough," Angelina stood on her tip toes to give Eli a kiss.

Eli retreated to his office on the other side of the house as Angelina made her way to their master bedroom. He shut the door behind him.

"Michael? I could really use you right now, buddy…"

He'd no sooner spoken the words out loud than Michael appeared before him.

"Wow. That may be the first time ever you've called on me directly like that."

"Had I known it would have been that simple I might have done it more often. I'm really desperate now, dude. What the hell is going on?"

"Can't tell you that."

"Well, what can you tell me, then?" Eli replied sarcastically.

"Easy, partner."

"Sorry. I'm a little anxious right now."

"Understandable. But everything is under control. You can't control what happens, you can only control how you react to what happens.

"That's comforting," Eli's sarcasm returned.

"It should be. It means all you have to focus on is your own next step."

"And what should that be?"

"Well, it's best if you figure that out for yourself…"

"Okay, give me a hint then?"

"To tell you the truth, I was going to pay you a visit tonight anyway."

"Oh?"

"Yes, you've been so busy lately you've neglected your purpose."

"My music is better than ever, Michael. And bringing Angelina into the show and onto the album has had a profound impact on people."

"True, true. You're on the right track there. Music is one part of your purpose, but remember the other?"

"Philanthropy?"

"Yes, but on a massive scale. Much bigger than what you're doing now. So big, that your current level of wealth could only scratch the surface of what is possible for you to accomplish. Remember what we talked about the last time I paid a visit?"

"Oh, shit. Cryptocurrencies. I checked the safe, Michael, I found my Bitcoin account. I have several million dollars in there. I just haven't done anything with it yet… my tour and the latest record is consuming me."

"Yes, I know. You must find balance again. You must save time for contemplating what to do with that money—

and how to create more of it. Do you remember what I told you, at the beginning of our relationship? In your past life, you signed a sacred contract with an organization known as Gemini, that holds you accountable to earning back nearly forty billion dollars of wealth in this lifetime."

"Oh, shit. I forgot about that."

"Do you remember also, that your karmic duty is to make right previous wrongs? And that one thing you did in your past life was to participate in a sex trafficking ring yourself?"

"I tried to forget about that."

"You can't run away from your responsibilities, Eli. They will not disappear on their own. Eventually, you will have to face them—whether in this lifetime, or the next. If you need to take some time off to honor these responsibilities, take it. Your career will not suffer from it. You should know that from experience."

"Okay, fine, I'll figure something out. But what does that have to do with the phone call? The phone call is why I called you here."

"Ah, yes. Who do you think called you?"

"I don't know, man. Is it about the sex trafficking ring?"

"Can't tell you that."

"Here we go again."

"Ask me a different question."

"Alright, was that article in the paper true? Did I really expose a massive, elite ring?"

"Can't answer that either."

"Agh, fuck."

"But what I can tell you is that there is a thriving, underground sex trafficking ring that is operating under everyone's noses."

"Even here in L.A.?"

"Yes, of course. It has a presence in nearly every major city, worldwide."

"Who is a part of this ring?"

"Some of the biggest names in your films, your music, your government. In fact, many of them are the same people who are controlling the banking system. Trust me, you don't want to know. But you don't need to bother yourself with that, anyway. You just need to focus on your next steps."

"I'd say I do need to bother with that—there is likely a bounty on my head!"

"Maybe so."

"You're really helping me feel better here, Michael."

"Well, I don't want to tell you sweet things just to make you feel better."

"Sometimes I wish you would."

Michael laughed. "I'll tell you what. I think it would be wise for you to lay low for a while. Get off the grid. Take some time off to reconnect with yourself, with others, and your purpose."

"And where should I do that?"

"Thailand might be nice."

"Is that a joke?

"No, not really. But since you're asking for my advice, I'd recommend you go somewhere else first."

"Yes…?"

"Have you heard of Burning Man?"

Eli laughed. "Burning Man? Isn't that where a bunch of hippies get naked and burn things in the desert?"

Michael chuckled. "It can be perceived as such. But there's so much more to it. It's an event built upon creative connection and community, decommodification and a gift economy. There is no exchange of currency at the event. Furthermore, to survive for a week under the harsh conditions of the desert, one must go within."

"That still sounds like a hippy festival."

"It's not, I assure you. A lot of tech industry elite go to Burning Man; they know it's a hotbed for innovation. You won't understand what it's really about until you experience it for yourself. Trust me, you will find answers to some of your questions there."

"Fair enough. You really think that's where I should go?"

"It's where you need to go. I've arranged a ticket for you. You just need to notify your pilot. The festival begins on Sunday. You've got two days to make other arrangements."

"What about Angelina?"

"She will be fine here. Have Ron stay with her. Or invite her. That's your call."

"At this Burning Man event…would I need security?"

Michael laughed. "No one will recognize you there. Wear silver paint and a skirt or something."

"What?"

"Never mind. Tell your assistant you're going to Burning Man, and to prepare your luggage. She will know what to do."

"Okay…"

"Have fun!" Michael grinned and left, as usual, just as suddenly as he came.

CHAPTER FIVE

THE DESERT

*B*urning *Man?! I can't believe he wants me to spend a week in the desert in the peak heat of summer,* Eli thought. Once again, he lay wide awake in the middle of the night. He was trying not to move much, as Angelina had finally fallen asleep beside him.

As strange as the proposition seemed, he had never known Michael to lead him into danger, nor to suggest any action that wasn't for his highest good. If Michael said that's where he needed to go to find answers, that's where he would go. *But should I take Angelina with me?* He decided to broach the subject with her first thing in the morning.

When he woke up after finally having fallen asleep around 4 a.m., Eli could hear Angelina in the kitchen. He threw on a T-shirt and joined her. She had just made her traditional breakfast juice of beetroot, celery, and kiwi. She had offered the drink to Ron, who stood sniffing the concoction and giving it a questionable look. Eli caught his reaction and laughed, despite his leftover anxiety from the night before. "Yeah, that was my first reaction too. But it's really not half bad, once you get used to it," Eli offered. "How was the night?" he added.

"Nothing alarming. Everything is under control." Ron and Eric had swapped shifts throughout the night, allowing each other some shuteye. "I wouldn't leave the house alone though for a few days—either of you. What are your schedules like today?"

Eli glanced over at Angelina.

"I have rehearsal, pretty much all day every day this week," she replied. "In fact, I should leave soon."

"I have a couple of planned media appearances today. Angelina…how important is it that you attend rehearsal later this week, and well, next week too?" Eli looked at her tentatively.

"How important? You know the business, Eli. It's very important. What are you getting at?"

"It's just…I have the feeling we should get out of town for a while. You know, lay low until all this blows over."

"That's not a bad idea," Ron concurred.

"I don't know…things are just starting to take off for me. I just got this role…"

"Your safety is most important," Eli interjected.

Angelina looked nervously at Eli. "I know. I'll think about it. Let's talk about it tonight. Right now, I've got to go." She reached for her purse.

"I'm sending Eric with you," Ron shared.

"Okay." Angelina leaned over and kissed Eli on the cheek. The lack of privacy made her self-conscious. "We'll talk more about this later, okay?"

"Okay. I love you," Eli returned her kiss and watched as Eric led her to the Toyota SUV with tinted windows in the driveway. *He probably has more time alone with her than I do now*, he thought, a bit jealously.

"I'm going to call my manager," Eli turned to Ron. "I'm leaving on Sunday for a week or so. I don't like canceling gigs, but I feel I have to this time. I'll have him say I'm sick and on voice rest or something."

Ron handed Eli his cell phone. "Here, use my phone. Just in case."

"Thanks," Eli reached for the phone and called his manager. Russ was not enthusiastic by any means about the request, but from the beginning of their relationship, Eli had made it clear that he called the shots.

"You should let me know where you're going," Ron stated firmly. "I'll go with you or arrange another team member to accompany you at all times."

"I...I'm going to Burning Man."

"That desert hippy festival in Nevada?"

"That's what I said."

"Why there? Never mind, it's not my job to question."

"Well, it's off the grid for one thing. It's easy to blend in. No one there should care who I am, and therefore want to kill me."

"You have a point."

"Anyway, it's not just for hippies. There's a lot of creative energy...a lot of innovative ideas are born there. Or, so I hear..." Eli was careful not to mention who he'd heard that from.

"Okay. Anyway, I should come with you. If Angelina stays here, I'll keep Eric on here with her."

Eli was caught off guard by a twinge of discomfort. The idea of another man, on duty or not, staying with Angelina in their home without him there gave him pause.

"Let's see...maybe she'll come with me. Anyway, Ron,

I think I'll only need you until I arrive at the festival. I'll be fine once I'm there."

"Are you sure?"

"Yes. I think your presence would attract attention to me. And I want to have an authentic experience there, anyway."

"Alright. It's up to you. But it makes me uncomfortable."

"I'll be fine."

Ron accompanied Eli to his press appearances that afternoon, but upon returning home late that night to find Angelina getting ready for bed, Eli asked Ron to afford them some privacy by staying in the lower level of the house.

Eli could feel Angelina's exhaustion.

"Are you alright, babe?" he asked.

"Yes, I am. I'm just tired. The director is really demanding. But I'm not complaining. I'm really grateful for how things are progressing."

"That's great, Ang," Eli joined her near the bed and held her in a warm embrace. "I'm really proud of you."

"Thanks," Angelina smiled.

Eli leaned forward and kissed her in a way that begged for her body.

"Not now, Eli," Angelina pulled back, a reaction entirely new to Eli.

"I thought it might help us relax and reconnect. It's been a stressful last few days…"

"I know, it's true, but I'm just so tired. And to be honest, it's awkward, knowing that Ron is here. It feels like we're under surveillance."

"I asked him to stay downstairs. It's completely private

up here."

"Still…"

Eli could feel an unusual emotional distance between them. She had never before rejected his body, which caused insecure voices in his head to consume him. *Is she still attracted to me? Has she met someone else? Is there some douchebag actor she's fallen for?* He suddenly felt sick to his stomach. He'd never felt jealousy like this before.

"Is everything okay with the film? You know, on the set?" He tried to tease information out of her.

"Yes, I told you, everything is fine. Actually, more than fine. I almost forgot to tell you…there's talk of submitting the film to Cannes. Can you imagine? My first screenplay going to Cannes?"

"Wow, Ang, that's amazing!" Eli was happy for her, but simultaneously even more insecure. With her success would come more fame…more money…more men.

"Are you sure? You don't look all that excited…"

"Of course, I'm excited for you. I just…how could you almost forget to tell me that?" Eli reverted to a childlike fear of being left out.

"You know how it has been, Eli. With the security issues, the newspaper, rehearsals…I have so much on my mind. Don't overthink it, babe, okay? Let's just get some rest."

"Okay. But…I wanted to talk to you about getting away. You said we'd talk about it tonight. Have you thought about it?"

"Honestly, no. I haven't. I'm sorry. Today was busier than I thought it would be. Can we talk about it tomorrow?"

"I've already made my decision. I'm going to Burning

Man. I'm leaving on Sunday."

"Burning Man?" Angelina looked confused.

"Yes, it's this festival in the desert, in Nevada."

"I know what it is, but I didn't know that was something you were interested in."

"Well…I wasn't. But…I just thought it would be a good place to get off the grid, you know? It feels safe to me now, with everything going on. Plus, I hear there are some really interesting people there, interesting ideas."

"Yes, I have friends that have gone. They loved it. But I can't take time off right now from work to go to a festival."

"It's not just about going to the festival, it's about getting away. You know, taking some time for us to be together."

"I don't know, Eli. I really can't blow this gig. How long were you thinking of being gone?"

"A little over a week."

"That's too long for me. The director would never go for that…"

"Can't you ask?"

"I can ask, but I know the answer. He just gave this big speech about how seriously we all need to take this commitment. He doesn't even want us to miss a day if we're sick."

"Well, you can at least try…"

"What I need now is to try to get some sleep…"

"Okay, but promise me you'll ask him tomorrow?"

"I promise we can talk more about this tomorrow."

"This is for our own safety, Angelina. And us. And the work we're here to do on this planet…"

Eli stopped just short of sharing that he'd had a visit from his guide the night before.

"This film is the work I'm here to do on this planet."

"But you can take a break and return to it. Like I have…"

"Your situation is different. You've reached the top of your career already; you call all the shots. I'm just getting started. There are sacrifices I have to make at this stage."

"But…"

"Eli, seriously. I need to sleep. I can't talk about this anymore right now. If you need an answer now, it's no, alright?" Angelina was losing patience; her voice rose to a level Eli had never heard before.

Are we having our first fight? Eli wondered. They'd had disagreements before, but they'd never yelled at each other.

"Fine. Don't come. Maybe it's best that way anyway," Eli matched her voice. He was aware that he sounded childish, but he was tired too. And he couldn't shake the stories in his head that something bigger was going on. That perhaps she didn't need him anymore.

"Goodnight, Eli," Angelina said softly. "Try to get some rest, okay? We both need it."

"Okay," Eli watched Angelina crawl into bed and switch the reading lamp off. He turned and went to the bathroom, shutting the door behind him. Splashing cold water on his face, he hoped to wash the insecure thoughts out of his head before he crawled into bed himself.

THE FOLLOWING DAY, Angelina did ask the director of the film for time off, but the most he would agree to was two days, which was not enough to make the trip worth it. When she returned home late that night to share the news with Eli, she was met with his feigned lack of interest.

"Fine," was all he'd said. Angelina could sense he didn't want to talk, and she understood that if she tried to press him to open up, what he would say would likely be something he would later regret saying, and she would prefer not to hear. She elected to give him space.

When they went to bed, Angelina placed her hand on the small of his back, but his pride would not allow him to reach out to her. What he couldn't articulate was that he supported her career and her decision, and what truly was still bothering him was the fact that she'd rejected his body the night before. He kept fearing that it had meant something more.

Anyway, he was okay with the fact that he would be going to Burning Man by himself. He didn't like leaving Angelina behind, but he was certain his security detail would take care of her safety. *That's all that guy Eric better do*, he thought to himself with disdain, aware that his sudden distrust in the man's personal agenda was completely unfounded.

Two days later, he and Ron boarded his private jet to Reno, Nevada. It was a three-hour drive from there to Black Rock City, the makeshift city in the desert that was built up and torn down every year by festival participants. A driver had been arranged to meet them at the airport. Eli had told his assistant back in L.A. that he'd wanted to blend in at the festival, so he was shocked when what the driver called an "art car" showed up as his means of transport.

The vehicle hardly resembled a car at all. He couldn't tell what model it had been in its former life, but whatever it was had been decked out with horns and wings and a metallic paint that produced rainbow reflections in the hot desert sun.

"I'm supposed to blend in arriving in *that*?!" he questioned the driver.

"Absolutely, sir. You will see."

Eli began to wonder what he'd gotten himself into.

"Are you going to wear that?" The driver motioned to

his jeans and T-shirt.

"I was planning on it…"

"I suggest you wear something a bit more…colorful. And you will need to protect your face—a pair of goggles and a hat and handkerchief should be sufficient."

He wasn't sure all of those items would be necessary, but he admitted they would do a good job of disguising his identity. He reached for his luggage to check what his assistant had packed for him. He was told that his accommodations upon arrival would be stocked with food and water and other comfort items, but his luggage contained his clothes.

He opened his suitcase and was met with an assortment of hats, feather boas, decorated loin cloths, beads, boots, goggles, a dust mask—clothes he would never have considered wearing on any other occasion. He reached for a rainbow-colored skirt.

"Like this?" he asked the driver.

"Now you're talking," the driver grinned, and Ron cracked up laughing.

Eli slipped the skirt on over his jeans and dropped his pants. He had to admit, the cool breeze on his man-parts felt nice. He turned back to the suitcase to find a shirt.

As if reading his mind, the driver suggested, "Don't even bother with a shirt. It's going to be hot."

Eli shook his head and stripped off his shirt, replacing it with the aforementioned protective accouterments, and got settled in the car for the drive. With a chuckle, he wondered if he looked more like a rock star now than he did in his performance clothes. But he trusted the advice of those who were more familiar with the event.

When the car finally pulled up to the gate—they'd encountered an enormous line that they'd agreed not to try to use his celebrity status to get him through—Eli understood why his assistant had packed his luggage the way she had. Everywhere he looked, people were decked out in costume. The car fit in, too.

The driver handed Eli a vehicle pass, festival ticket, and directions to his campsite, where he'd find "a comfortable RV for his stay." According to prior-made arrangements, the driver would be taking Ron back to Reno in a separate vehicle. The "art car" was for Eli's use.

"Are you sure you want to be on your own here, Eli?" Ron asked.

Eli glanced around at the fairies, warlocks, and lord knows what else around him. He felt primed for adventure. "Yes, absolutely." It was liberating to not travel with an entourage and to draw less attention than the wildly-dressed attendees that surrounded him.

"Alright, man. I'll see you back to Reno next Monday."

"Thanks, Ron." Eli shook Ron's hand and generously tipped the driver before driving the mandatory five miles per hour through the gate and to his campsite.

The whole Burning Man site was around seven square miles and situated on a dried-up lake bed. Most of the site was open space, but a significant portion was reserved for campsites, which were arranged in a sort of giant wheel; it's clock-like design also served as a functional address system. At the opening of the circle was the Burning Man symbol—a wooden sculpture of "the man," to be burned on the final night of the event. For a first-timer, the design could be substantially confusing.

"Alright, now what?" Eli said to himself. Everyone else seemed to have arrived in a group. He drove slowly, looking for signs as to where he was in the circle. Just then, a beautiful blonde woman dressed only in panties and beads around her neck waved him over to her. *Oh god, does she recognize me?* Eli wondered. *Maybe this is just like one of my shows after all.*

"Hey!" She called. "Is this your first time at the playa?"

"Uhh…I guess so," Eli assumed she meant the festival. He tried not to look at her breasts, which hung before him as she bent down to talk to him through the car window. He had to admit the woman was beautiful, but he tried to focus on what she was telling him.

"I thought so. You looked lost. Can I help?"

"Uh, yeah." Eli fumbled with the map he'd been given, which had a red X where his campsite was. "Do you know where this is?"

"Yes, we're not far from there now. See over there?" she gestured. "That's my dome. Just beyond it, there is a blue flag. Your spot should be close to there."

"Thank you," Eli nodded.

"Anytime!" The girl danced off, leaving a cloud of dust in her wake.

Eli drove the car forward a few hundred feet and pulled into the reserved space his assistant had arranged. He was pleased with the Classic Airstream RV in its spot. As soon as he parked, he was approached by a group of men and women in gold body paint. "Welcome!" They called. "Do you need any help unloading?"

Eli knew he could handle it on his own, but he'd become accustomed to having a porter, and this was the next best thing. "Sure, thanks a lot." A couple of men unloaded his luggage from the car as the women gazed about the RV.

"Wow, this is incredible!"

Eli felt slightly embarrassed by the luxury of his accommodations. He took a look around himself. It had a queen-sized bed, a full kitchen, and the all-important air conditioning. *So, it's not completely an authentic Burning Man experience*, Eli considered, looking about at his neighbors, who were setting up tents. *I guess I've become a bit spoiled.*

He thanked the group, who had not asked for his name and made no sign of having recognized him, as they returned to their own camp. Eli considered offering to help them as well but the intense afternoon heat had made him tired. Amid the flurry of activity around him, he decided to lay up in his private space and take a nap until the weather cooled.

He opened the windows to let in a breeze, although he quickly realized he'd have to close them again to avoid dust layering over everything inside. He turned on the AC instead. Stretching out on the bed, his thoughts led to Angelina. He was sorry to have left her in the state that he had; they'd hardly had any opportunity to connect since their…fight?…two nights before. He'd wanted to talk with her about his concerns, but Angelina had been too tired by the time she got home.

It didn't take long for Eli to fall asleep, and he slept longer than intended. It was after 8 p.m. when he woke to some commotion at a nearby camp. He threw his skirt back on—he still couldn't believe what he was wearing—and stepped outside the RV.

"Hey! Over here!" He saw the blonde woman he'd met earlier motion to him. "We're building a temple. Come join us!"

Eli wandered over to their gathering. What already stood before him was breathtaking. A straw sculpture was taking form, which was starting to resemble the Taj Mahal.

"Whoa, you guys made that?!"

"Yes," the girl answered. "Well, Daniel designed it. We're just helping put the pieces together."

At that moment, a tall and slender man with a shaved head came over to him. "Hi, I'm Daniel. And don't listen to her—this is a collective effort. We all are playing an important part in its creation."

"Well, it looks fantastic," Eli acknowledged.

"Do you want to help us? We could use another hand."

"Yeah, sure. Just tell me what to do. I'm…Eli, by the way." He decided his clothing did enough to mask his real identity.

"Welcome, Eli. This is Charlie, Matt, Kari, and Alicia." The latter was the blonde woman he'd met.

"Nice to meet you all."

Over the next several hours, the group worked together to complete the temple. They were joined by additional people as the night went along, but not once did anyone ask where anyone was from, or what they did for a job. All of the typical social rituals didn't seem to apply at Burning Man. Eli was grateful for that. "I think this is going to be a fun week," he said to himself.

ELI THOUGHT HE'D experienced the peak of sensory overload while performing on stage various times, but being on stage was nothing compared to what he experienced at Burning Man over the next several days. Every direction he looked was a feast for the senses. Whatever one could imagine, could be created in the desert.

Larger-than-life art sculptures of the most diverse variety met his eyes. What people called "mutant vehicles"—

methods of transportation decorated even beyond the more traditional "art car" level—were driven across the sand. People wore eclectic costumes that ranged from nothing but body paint to full regalia of the feathered, furry, and shiny kind. There was a fair share of nudity as well; sometimes it was difficult for Eli not to indulge in appreciating all of the beautiful women's bodies.

Stimulation at the event wasn't limited to the visual; music was played live, using traditional and non-traditional instruments alike. The smell of thousands of sweaty bodies permeated the air. The intensity of the sun's rays simultaneously exhausted Eli and inspired him to stay active, so as to distract himself from his body's discomfort.

He could understand now what Michael had meant by desert conditions causing him to go within. He met many fascinating people at the festival; he spent countless hours in conversation with attendees from very different walks of life than his own. However, at times he secluded himself in his RV to afford himself the luxury of self-reflection.

The event itself was deeply enriching, as were the conversations he'd had with others, but he couldn't figure out how his being there was meant to answer the questions he had asked Michael. How was this event supposed to lead him to his purpose in life?

Sometimes, he paid that question no attention. Halfway through the week, he felt his temptations tested. He was sitting in a circle, enjoying a beer with the neighboring camp. He seldom drank alcohol anymore, but the event's culture of freedom from restrictions relaxed the expectations he'd placed on himself over the past year. Relaxing that one constraint, however, caused the floodgates open.

The group held a cookout, and the smell of grilled meat

wafted through the desert air.

"Care for a burger, Eli?"

Angelina isn't here to judge me, Eli considered, forgetting that she had never told him what to do or not do. "Yeah, serve one up!" he answered, feeling like a child let loose in a candy store.

It was the best burger he ever tasted. Feeling on cloud nine, Eli reached for another beer. *No rules, tonight.* Eli grinned. The evening rolled on; Charlie retrieved a guitar from his tent and played folk tunes as passerby joined their gathering. A sing-a-long turned into a full-on dance party. Eli wasn't much of a dancer himself, but it was clear nobody here cared what they looked like. He flailed around like the rest of them. *This must be what Woodstock felt like. I always wished I could have been there!* He smiled to himself.

As the night progressed, he let go of himself further. A theme of the event was radical self-expression, and he could see it played out everywhere he turned. Bodies danced and generated even more heat, while more clothing came off. As more people joined in, the closer the bodies grew to each other. Thoughts of Angelina were not absent from his mind, but they had turned resentful.

She probably hasn't even thought about me since I left, Eli thought. *She's too busy for me now.* A background voice in his mind reminded him that he was often too busy for her, too, but he brushed it aside. He brought his thoughts back to the present and allowed himself to take in all of the women around him. They were carefree, high-spirited, devoid of self-consciousness. *Damn, they are beautiful*, he smiled. Just then, his eyes met Alicia's gaze. He'd admired the curves of her body before, but in his open state of mind, they were now highlighted.

She winked at him. He grinned back. All of the women on the road he had passed by since committing to Angelina came to mind now. He'd been allured by their beauty as well, but not like this. Those women had been attracted to Eli Evans, the rock star. These women here saw him as a fellow participant, a co-creator of this amazing energy that only those here, right now, could fully understand. If his gaze had fallen upon another woman there at that moment, hers would likely have been the body he would have been drawn to. As it was, it was Alicia's.

She danced over to him, floating like an angel. Her light and freckled skin appeared exotic, just as Angelina's dark skin had when he'd first laid his eyes upon it. It's not that he loved Angelina any less at that moment; it was that he craved validation—that he was still young, still free. Still a man.

"Isn't it crazy to think about?" Alicia smiled inquisitively at Eli.

"What?" Eli grinned back.

"How, in a couple of days, all of this will cease to exist. *Poof.* As if none of it was ever here, and none of this even happened…"

"It is…" Eli answered although he hadn't thought much about it until that moment. *Impermanence. Nothing in life is made to last forever.*

Her body pressed up against his. In the spirit of the night, his outfit was down to nothing but a loincloth; hers was completely naked. Both were covered in sweat and sand, but that only contributed to the rawness of the moment. Alicia's hands softly graced Eli's chest, making their way over his shoulders and down his back. His lips met hers as his fingers lightly traced her nipples before he bent down and placed his lips over them as if to drink from her fountain of youth.

He felt her loosen the ties around his waist that held the only piece of modesty left on this body. The cloth fell to the ground, and whatever hesitation or indiscretion that may have crossed his mind faded away with the awareness that couples danced all around him, satiating themselves with the same joy of freedom and sexual expression that he now participated in. *God, this feels good,* he allowed himself to melt into the moment and into the night.

ELI SUSPECTED HE might wake up with regret the next morning. But he did not. He felt alive. He knew that what had happened the night before was what had to happen, although he wasn't sure why. He also knew that the connection he'd had with Alicia was meant to be fleeting—it was understood among them both. It was simply an exchange of physical, anonymous love, at a level that was non-committal and non-emotional.

Interestingly, however, the experience made him miss Angelina. He wanted to tell her about it, as absurd as he thought that sounded. He wanted to discuss what he learned about himself—he'd been feeling neglected and stifled. Perhaps they were self-created emotions, but he knew they were based on actual circumstances in their relationship. *Some things need to change*, he admitted, although he wasn't sure he knew exactly what.

He feared her reaction if he decided to bring the subject up to her—which he felt he had no choice but to do. He knew he would be irate if she were to tell him she'd been with another man. *She might leave me*, he considered, as a wave of discomfort washed over him.

Any further reflection would have to wait, however. The camp was starting to spring to life. He'd just finished showering and getting dressed—today's costume of choice was a fringed leather jacket and matching pants. His hair had become long enough to be pulled back into a short ponytail, which he topped with a jester's hat as he reached for his goggles—which were convenient both for keeping the dust out of his eyes and for self-disguise.

"Eli! You in there? There's someone here I think you should meet." Daniel called out to him while rapping on his door.

Eli wiped his face with a handkerchief, unlocked the door and stepped outside.

"Hey man, this is Jeff. Jeff, Eli. I figured you two should meet after that conversation we had about cryptos the other night."

Eli, Daniel, and a number of others from a nearby camp had gotten into a discussion a couple of nights prior about Bitcoin and other cryptocurrencies. Eli had mentioned he had Bitcoin totaling a substantial amount and was beginning to develop an interest in learning how to mine for more—and to use those funds for philanthropic efforts.

"Nice to meet you, Eli."

"The pleasure is mine." Eli vaguely recognized the man from various media appearances. He knew he was a high-roller in the cryptocurrency world.

"Daniel was filling me in on some of your ideas around how to use digital currencies to fund development efforts in third-world countries. Would you like to join me and some of my buddies for a cookout to discuss that topic further?"

"I'd love to," Eli nodded.

"Great, come along with me now, if you'd like."

Eli hopped in Jeff's vehicle and was led behind the façade of an art exhibit to luxury accommodations on the outskirts of the festival grounds. A pop-up village had been created; a collection of heavily-equipped RVs and impermanent outdoor shade-structures dotted the community. A gourmet meal was being prepared by a hired chef.

Eli was introduced to several Silicon Valley elites, many of whom he recognized as being key players in highly-successful startups. He discovered he'd been recognized as well; Jeff introduced him as Eli Evans, so he knew he was not anonymous in this circle.

The discussions that followed expanded his mind beyond any he'd held previously. He learned insider tips about how to mine for Bitcoins, but he learned so much beyond that. He was told that the topics covered should be kept entirely private, as they contained sensitive information that if released would mean the failure of their proposed enterprise.

The main topic discussed was joining forces to rebuild Puerto Rico, which had been devastated by a recent hurricane, using digital currencies. Jeff and his colleagues had reason to believe that the U.S. dollar and the central banking system were on the verge of total collapse and that real wealth could only be obtained through cryptocurrencies.

If that's true, I have a lot to lose, Eli considered. *But I also have a lot to gain—as do those currently living in poverty.*

Eli returned to his camp that night rife with ideas. He had met many bigwigs over the years but never had they spoken of such earnest attempts to use their wealth for the greater good in such ways. These elite men and women may enjoy high standards of living for themselves, but they also believed in their opportunity to play a key role in redistributing wealth so that more people could enjoy living beyond basic survival mode.

"Thanks, Michael," Eli spoke out loud. "I'm glad I came here." The following night, however, Eli wasn't as convinced he should have come.

ELI AWOKE LATE the next morning, having rested deeply the night before. The connections he'd made with the tech industry leaders were still foremost on his mind. *I have the opportunity to help lead entire countries out of poverty*, he marveled to himself. He'd already made plans to attend high-profile meetings in San Francisco after he returned. The men knew Eli was an influencer, and they'd been eager to bring him onboard their project.

But first, Burning Man had yet to reach its peak. Energy in the encampment was high, anticipating the official burning of the forty-foot tall, wooden sculpture known as "the man" later that night. To some, the effigy represented everything the festival stood against, including consumerism and the central banking industry.

We can put a stop to the latter, Eli thought as he rose out of bed and began to cook a warm breakfast of eggs and toast. As the eggs cooked, he stretched his arms overhead, an act that reminded him it had been quite a while since he'd practiced yoga. With him and Angelina on different schedules, he'd been less motivated to stick to his exercise routine—and at Burning Man, there was no such thing as routine.

He settled into a quiet meal in solitude before which he said gratitude and set an intention to take better care of his physical body after he returned home. *I'm going to go right back onto the road, however*, he realized. The home he'd purchased with dreams of a never-ending future with Angelina suddenly felt very far away. *Is she even happy there? Is she happy with me anymore?* He wondered. His insecurities came rushing back after having been on hiatus with all of the distractions at the festival.

After breakfast and before the heat of the day kicked in, Eli decided to go for a walk and check out the various art installations one last time before they'd all be dismantled and taken away in accordance with the event's "leave no trace" philosophy. He put on that day's disguise —silver face paint, sunglasses, a wide-brimmed hat and yet another funky outfit his assistant had packed for him.

Along the way, he was offered an assortment of gifts—a foot massage, a handmade bracelet, a poem, and a condom. *Perhaps I should have used one of these last night,* he considered about the latter. Rather than think about Alicia, however, he thought about Angelina. He predicted that finding time for intimacy with her wouldn't get any easier when he returned to his tour. *Her schedule is only going to get crazier as her film progresses,* Eli thought. *And as she becomes more and more famous.* He knew that once the film was done, she'd be flooded with media appearances as part of a heavy publicity campaign.

Eli's thoughts had distracted him to the extent that he hadn't even noticed there were no more art exhibits in the area. And after two hours of walking around in the heat of the desert, he was incredibly thirsty. *That's okay, I'll just ask someone I meet along the way for something to drink,* he thought. He'd become accustomed to the generous, gifting culture of the event.

Unbeknownst to him, however, he had walked so far that he was off Burning Man grounds. Not many people were in sight. *Shit*, he thought. *Where am I?* His urge to panic was interrupted when a man with dreadlocks called over to him, "Hey, man! You thirsty?"

That was timely, he thought. Eli turned his gaze over to the man. He was carrying a tray with holes in it, stocked with drinks.

"I've got iced tea and beer. What's your pleasure?"

"Thanks, man. Iced tea would be fantastic," Eli answered.

"You got it."

Eli removed a handkerchief from his pocket and wiped the sweat off his brow. The face paint made him extra hot, but it was worth it to be able to go unrecognized.

The man handed him a glass of tea. "Drink up," he toasted Eli's glass with his own and proceeded to gulp the tea down. Eli followed suit, but he stopped after a few sips.

"Is this sweet tea?" He asked. He knew the added sugar could dehydrate him in these conditions.

"Oh, yeah, I mean, I added just a little bit of sugar. Is something wrong?"

Eli didn't want to appear ungrateful. "No man, it's okay. I just should get back to camp anyway. Thanks for the drink though, I appreciate it." He knew he'd need to rehydrate with water, and there was something about the guy's nervous reaction that made Eli slightly uncomfortable and not wanting to stick around.

"Are you sure you don't want the rest of your drink?"

"No man, I'm cool. Thanks again," Eli walked off. It took him another two hours to make it back to his camp, passing on invitations along the way. He was sure he could have asked any of the nearby campers for water, but the sunlight was straining his eyes and he was starting to get a headache and a little nauseous, and what he really wanted was to lie down in a quiet space.

The afternoon heat was at its peak. Eli was incredibly grateful for the small air conditioner in his RV. He cranked it up, washed the paint and dust off his face, drank a tall glass of water, and laid down to rest. He may have continued sleeping throughout the night, had a pounding on his door that evening not awoken him.

"Eli! Are you in there?" A female voice called.

Eli chalked up his loss of balance when stumbling out of bed to having just woken up. He reached absentmindedly for the door. He recognized Alicia before him, but the shape of her body moved slightly with his vision.

"Are you coming with us? Everyone else has already left. You're going to miss the burning of the man!" She asked, taken aback a bit by seeing him without his face paint.

"Huh?" For a moment, Eli had forgotten where he was. As his vision centered, he saw the desert dust floating around them and remembered Burning Man.

"Are you okay?" Alicia asked, with a look of concern.

"Yeah, yeah. Just a bit dizzy. I'm coming." He stepped down from the RV and shut the door behind him.

As the two walked toward the epicenter of the event, Eli struggled to walk in a straight line. Alicia looked at him strangely, a combination of confusion over his unusual behavior and a curious feeling of having seen him before. They reached the wooden sculpture, which was already shrouded in flames.

"Can you believe there are 70,000 people here?" Alicia asked innocently. "I never could have imagined so many people in one place before."

Eli phased in and out of consciousness. "Actually, I

can..." his voice trailed off. *I've filled stadiums of more than that,* he thought with a trace of ego, before all clarity in his thoughts faded. He felt as if he were sleepwalking, in a dream state.

"Eli?" He heard his name being spoken. He saw Alicia's mouth move slowly, in the form of his name.

"Yes?"

"Are you sure you're okay? You look distracted."

"I just..." Eli collapsed into the dirt, causing dust to float all around his motionless body.

CHAPTER SIX

LOVE LESSONS

Eli would have no memory of the course of events that took place next, but what he discovered when he woke two days later was that he'd been airlifted from Burning Man to a hospital in Reno. If he was disoriented during the burning of the man, he was equally so upon waking to find himself in a hospital bed with tubes along his arms and no one recognizable in view.

"Hello?" Eli called out.

"Ah, you're awake!" A nurse's gentle voice was heard before she was seen, after pulling back a privacy curtain. "How are you feeling, Eli?" she asked.

"I...I don't know. Where am I?"

"You're in Reno. You've been here in the hospital for two days. You gave us quite a scare, but you're recovering well."

"Recovering...from what, exactly?"

"I'll let the doctor explain. You have a guest as well. She just stepped out to use the restroom, but she should be back soon. She'll be so happy to see you awake!"

Just then, Angelina walked in the room. "Eli! Oh, thank

God!" She rushed to his bedside and planted a kiss on his lips as she rested her hand on his forehead. "My love, how are you? I was so worried…"

"Angelina…" he whispered.

"Yes, yes, I am here. I flew in as soon as I heard the news. Ron is here, too. He's in the lobby. And your parents are on their way—they're driving down from Oregon."

"What happened?" Eli asked.

"You…well, I'll let the doctor explain."

"Everyone keeps saying that…where's the doctor?" Eli asked, his voice scratchy.

"I'll go get him now," the nurse made her way down the hallway.

Eli squeezed Angelina's hand with the little strength he had. "Thank you…"

"For what?" Angelina kissed him again.

"For being here."

"Of course! You don't need to thank me for that. I love you."

"But…your film…"

"Everything is taken care of. We'll return home together and I'll resume my work. But for now, just focus on getting well. Oh, I'm so glad to see you!"

The doctor entered the room. "Eli, great to see you awake. How are you feeling?" He went about checking Eli's vitals.

"I've felt better. Please, tell me what's going on."

The doctor stole a glance at Angelina as if asking for permission. She nodded.

"You had poison in your system, Eli."

"Poison? What kind of poison?"

"Belladonna. It's a toxic plant."

Eli had heard of it. His aunt, who had studied medicinal plants, had warned him about the dangers of the plant that grew in some parts of the United States. "That's absurd. How is that possible?"

"That's a very good question. When you are feeling better, we have several questions for you about how you spent your last hours before you collapsed."

"I collapsed?"

"Yes, at Burning Man. A number of individuals and paramedics were involved in your air evacuation. They saved your life."

Eli released a long sigh. *Burning Man*. He had almost forgotten. Now, it felt like a dream.

"We immediately induced vomiting upon your arrival. To remove toxins, we applied a suspension of activated carbon. You showed vast improvement after your system was emptied. Belladonna poisoning can be deadly, but the amount you ingested was below your body's threshold."

"I…I still don't understand. I don't know how…" Eli's heart rate showed an increase on the machine.

"There will be time for reflection and an investigation later. It's important that you rest for now," the doctor insisted. "In fact, visiting hours are over as well. Angelina…" the doctor gestured toward the door.

"The doctor is right, Eli. You need your rest. Please, don't try to figure everything out now. I'll be in the lobby. I'll call your parents." Angelina squeezed his hand and made her way out of the room.

"You should be able to go home by tomorrow," the doctor turned toward Eli. "Rest now."

Eli's eyes were indeed getting heavy. He welcomed the peace left in the room with the doctor's exit.

Eli's parents arrived later that night to find Eli more awake and coherent. Carol kissed his head and held his hand. "Eli, it's so good to see you." Robert placed his hand on Eli's shoulder. "Son," his eyes glazed over with tears.

"Mom, Dad. You shouldn't have come all this way."

"You're our son. Of course, we would come. How are you feeling?" Carol asked.

"Tired…sore…but getting better. The doctor says I should have a full recovery within two weeks."

"That's great news. But…what happened?" His dad asked. "How did you get belladonna in your system?"

"Honestly…I'm not sure. But I have an idea…"

"Yes?" his dad further inquired.

"I accepted a glass of iced tea from a guy at the festival…it tasted sweet. The guy said he put sugar in it, but the doctor says belladonna has a sweet flavor. It could have been that…I don't know."

"Why on earth would he have wanted to poison you? And what were you doing drinking something from a stranger?" Carol's motherly instincts kicked in.

"Everything is shared at Burning Man, Mom. There's a level of trust there that doesn't exist outside of the festival."

"Well, look where trust got you…Where was your bodyguard?" Robert added.

"He didn't come with me. I'm not even sure if that was what had the toxin. There's no way to know for sure."

"Well, I'm glad you're okay," Carol tried to shift the subject; she didn't want to upset Eli when he should be focused on his recovery.

"Yes, the doctor says I can go home tomorrow. I'll be on bed rest for a week or so, but at least I'll be out of here."

"Would you like us to stay with you while you recover? We can meet you in L.A," Carol suggested.

"No, no. What about the farm? And besides, I'll be okay. I'll hire help."

"Are you sure? We could hire help for the farm, instead," his dad chimed in.

"Don't worry about it. I'll be fine," it occurred to Eli that with the strange phone call he'd received a couple of weeks ago and now a potential attempted poisoning, his property would remain on high-security alert. He didn't want his parents to stay in that type of environment; they would only worry more about him.

"Well, let us know if you change your mind…" Carol smiled at her son. "We don't want to exhaust you. We've booked a hotel nearby so that we can see you off tomorrow. We will let you rest for the night."

"Thanks, Mom. Thanks for coming you guys."

"Next time, we hope to see you under more pleasurable circumstances," his dad said lovingly, but Eli couldn't help but feel a twinge of guilt that he hadn't seen them since Christmas, nearly eight months before. "We love you, Son."

"I love you both, too."

ELI FLEW HOME on his private jet the following morning. A medic went with him, along with Ron and Angelina. Carol and Robert hugged their son tightly outside of the plane. "Take care of yourself. Remember, we're always here for you if you need us," Carol kissed him on the cheek.

It was only a ninety-minute flight home. He mostly remained quiet, his gaze out the window. Angelina held his hand the whole way there. He could feel her unconditional love. *I'm going to have to tell her about the week soon,* he thought. He hadn't always been completely open with her in the past, and he wanted to change that. *For better or for worse, I'm going to be honest about everything.*

Eli was assisted out of the plane and into a car that was driven the rest of the way home. The sound of the waves and the smell of salt was a refreshing change from the desert air. *And way better than the hospital room*, he considered.

He thought back to his experience at Burning Man. He had heard the event could be life-changing, and in some ways, he suspected that it was for him. He was inspired by all of the art and creativity, and the epic scale of what could be built and torn down in merely a matter of days. He regretted that he hadn't been there to witness the disassembly of the event—to see what it looked like and felt like when what had appeared permanent ceased to exist. He already had a song about that concept brewing in his head.

And, he was excited about the relationships he'd formed there. Most were, like the event itself, impermanent. He likely would never see or hear from any of the other participants again—no contact information, or even last names, had been exchanged. However, he did have ways to get in contact with Jeff and the other tech billionaires he'd met. He couldn't wait to learn more about their endeavors with cryptocurrencies and get involved with rebuilding Puerto Rico. When he recovered fully, Jeff would be the first person he'd call to arrange a meeting in Silicon Valley.

He was also contemplative about the idea of sex without love. He'd had plenty on the road prior to his relationship with Angelina, but could it fulfill more than simply the physical need he'd experienced on the road? Could it somehow contribute to his own evolution? He wasn't sure he could articulate it to Angelina or anyone else in a way that made sense, but he felt that he'd grown as a person after his experience with Alicia. It reminded him that he did have freedom of choice—that he was only ever held back by the constraints he placed on himself.

Sharing those thoughts with Angelina equally excited him and scared him. How would she react? The last thing he wanted to do was hurt her. He could see by the way she was immediately by his side when he was sick that she did still care for him deeply. He realized that so many of the thoughts he'd had prior to the festival had been a result of his own insecurities.

He chose a moment after dinner to address the subject. He had just started to be able to digest solid foods, and they'd shared a simple meal of rice and steamed vegetables.

"Angelina?"

"Yes?"

"How was your time while I was away?"

"Oh, you know. Busy. Long days on the set."

"Ron said everything was fine, security-wise, while I was gone."

"Yes, Eric made sure I arrived to work and back home safely and watched over the house. I must admit, it was kind of annoying to have him around so much though," she laughed.

"Really?"

"Yeah. My drives used to be my quiet time, you know? He kept to himself at the house though. I was hardly at home anyway."

Eli realized how silly it had been to worry about Eric breaking his professionalism to try anything with Angelina. Ron only hired the best.

"Do you want to hear more about the festival?"

"Yes, of course. I was waiting until you felt up to sharing your experience with me. How was it?"

"Well, it ended pretty miserably."

"I can imagine…"

"But up until that last night, it was amazing. It was so beautiful to be surrounded by such a sense of creativity and community."

Angelina smiled. "Yes, I've heard stories from friends about it. It sounds incredible. Maybe if things calm down with the film, I can go next year."

"I met some really interesting people."

"Tell me about them."

"Well, I was introduced to some powerful people in the cryptocurrency world. I learned a lot about how to mine for Bitcoin. I think I can actually do it myself."

"That's great. But what would be your reason for doing that?"

"That's the thing…these guys have some really big ideas. I won't go into detail, but in essence, they have a plan for rebuilding Puerto Rico. I mean, using all solar-powered energy and a foundation of really sustainable infrastructure. Of course, it will take a lot of money that the country itself doesn't have. But that's what's so exciting…I can contribute to that effort substantially with the Bitcoin money I mine."

"That sounds wonderful. You know you have my support in any way possible."

Eli smiled. "You're amazing, you know that?"

Angelina giggled. "Well, I don't feel so amazing lately. I've been so busy that I'm afraid I haven't had much time for you or my family or anything else in life except my career. But, I keep telling myself that it's temporary and that it's for the greater good in the end. I know this film will help a lot of people."

"I know the feeling. I understand. But, babe?"

"Yes?"

"I didn't understand everything before the festival. I mean, I knew you had—and still have—a lot on your plate with the film. But…I felt that perhaps you weren't as committed to being together anymore. I felt…a bit rejected, to be honest."

"What gave you that idea?" Angelina was surprised.

"You made no effort for intimacy. You were always too tired, even just to talk…about the trip to Burning Man, for example."

Angelina waited to make sure he was finished with his thought before replying. "That's true. I was too tired for anything, and I probably will be for quite some time once I go back to the set tomorrow. It's not personal though, Eli. Honestly. You know I love you."

Even though Eli suspected as much by this time, it was still nice to hear her say those words.

"You know, Eli…" Angelina was searching for the right words. "We…we can't be each other's everything."

"What do you mean?"

"I mean…I can't be responsible for giving you everything that you need. Sometimes, I'll be emotionally unavailable. Or physically unavailable. We each have to take responsibility for our own needs, and not depend on each other to…complete us. Have you read Gary Zukav's book, *Seat of the Soul?*"

"No…"

"In it, he talks about spiritual partnerships, as opposed to the socially-constructed idea most people have about relationships or marriage, which is built upon an ancient archetype. In this new archetype, commitment, compassion, courage, and conscious communication are the four main requirements for a spiritual partnership—and I don't mean commitment to each other."

"Then commitment to what?"

"To our own spiritual growth."

"I'm not sure I understand…"

"The traditional model of partnership actually encourages emotional distance, because if there's any dissent among the couple, historically, their survival was threatened. In a spiritual partnership, the energy dynamic is very different. The couple isn't just working towards common goals in regard to providing for their family and so forth, but towards each member becoming self-aware—learning what their feelings, thoughts, intentions, fears, and loves are. Discovering what it means to be you, or to be me, in this life."

Angelina paused long enough to allow Eli time to assimilate that message before continuing.

"When I entered into a relationship with you, I did so because I could feel that we were both committed to our higher purposes. We each wanted to make a difference in the world, in a big way, and I could feel how we could complement each other in those efforts. We could help each other reach higher than we could have alone, you know? I…I didn't think you wanted me to be your everything."

"I guess I hadn't thought about our relationship like that. I thought you…needed me, I guess. As my partner."

"Needed you for what exactly?"

"I don't know…to provide for you, for one thing. To be a man for you."

"I've never needed you to provide for me, Eli. This house is amazing…it's beautiful. But I don't need it. I am perfectly capable of supporting myself at a level that's aligned with my own income, and I would be happy doing so."

"Are you happy living here?"

"Of course! I love living here with you, Eli. But I would love living with you in a small house in the middle of nowhere, too. I saw the joy this house brought you, however, when we were looking for a home, so I supported your decision and rolled with it."

"Am I...satisfying your other needs? As a man, I mean?"

"First of all, again, you don't need to satisfy any of my needs. But if you're asking if I'm happy with the physical intimacy you provide me with, of course! I only wish I could take advantage of your sexy body more," Angelina playfully bit Eli's neck.

Eli wanted to respond to her play, but the pressure of what he was about to tell her weighed heavily upon him.

"I...I have something to tell you, and I'm quite afraid to do it, to be honest..."

"Go ahead, be honest."

"Before I left for Burning Man...I wasn't in the right headspace. I had ideas about...us. I thought you might be unhappy with me, and I was starting to feel resentful."

"About what?"

"It sounds ridiculous now, but like you were trying to keep me from being who I am...or from being free."

"Eli, I would never hold either of those intentions."

"Well, I needed to feel free again, anyway. In charge of my own life and body. To remember who I am without you for a bit."

"We all need to feel that way sometimes."

"We do?"

"Absolutely. We can't ever risk losing ourselves in a relationship. We have to constantly check in with ourselves—and each other—to make sure that we're following the path we're each meant to follow. Sometimes it's not the same path."

"But can our paths...diverge for just a brief moment in time, and then come right back together, without negative consequences?"

"What are you getting at?"

"Angelina, I...I slept with someone at Burning Man."

Angelina sat quietly, letting his statement in. Eli felt his body break out in a sweat, and his heart rate increased with each passing second. Her silence lasted what felt like an eternity before she asked, "Tell me more about it."

Eli swallowed; his mouth had become dry. "I know it sounds cliché, but it just happened. Everyone...hundreds of us were swept up in this moment of connection and...and love. Not romantic love, but a different kind of love. Love for life, really. Love for our bodies and the sensations they can create. Love for...all of humanity." Eli looked into Angelina's eyes to try to discern what she was thinking, what she was feeling.

"That's beautiful."

"Wait, what?" Eli wasn't sure he'd heard her right.

"If that's what the experience meant to you, then I'm happy for you. That's a feeling some people never allow themselves to feel."

"You mean...you're not mad?"

"I'm certainly not mad. How could I be? That would be like punishing you—or anyone—for appreciating the beauty of what it means to be human."

"So, you're not hurt then?"

"I didn't say that. After all, I am only human too. It

takes a very highly evolved soul not to feel jealousy on one occasion or another, and I'm not there yet. But I'm trying to get there. Actually, that is what I was trying to say earlier—if we agree that our partnership is a spiritual one, then you just offered me a great gift."

"I'm not sure I follow…"

"You've given me an opportunity to practice not feeling jealous. To respond with love, rather than fear."

"That's deep."

"I suppose it is." Angelina smiled, though a tear fell from one of her eyes. Eli reached over to her and kissed it away.

"I never meant to hurt you," he said.

"I know. And anyway, you can't make me feel hurt no matter what you do. In the end, it's my choice."

"Do you know what?"

"You are the greatest gift that has ever happened to me."

"Actually, Eli, I think your parents are the greatest gift that's ever happened to you. But I'll accept a close second," she said with a wink.

He pulled her in for a tight hug—as tight as he could with all of the energy he could surmount.

CHAPTER SEVEN

THE INVESTIGATION

Eli's recovery took a full two weeks, but it was not time wasted. He took advantage of the break from touring to become adept at mining for Bitcoin. With what he'd learned from Jeff and the other tech billionaires at Burning Man and through additional conference calls after his return, he was able to begin personal mining.

First, he had to invest in specialized hardware, built using application specific integrated circuit (ASIC) chips designed for mining. The cost of the hardware was high, as would be running it, but the expense did not phase Eli. He knew it would generate a return. He used the hardware to run the software Jeff had recommended, day and night. The software's job was to force the system to complete complicated calculations in order to mine, or create new Bitcoins, to add to general circulation. The miner is paid a transaction fee for those new Bitcoins, and Eli's sophisticated system was already making him an even richer man.

The process was somewhat technical, but it reminded him of how much he'd loved math as a child. To him, mining for Bitcoin was reminiscent of piecing together notes to create a song. He was further inspired by what he could do with the money he made in the process. *This is all going to Puerto Rico, for starters*, he thought. He had joined a coalition with Jeff and his colleagues to channel the money towards new infrastructure in the country. Roads were already being built, using recycled plastic rather than oil-based bitumen. Power was being generated using solar energy. New wind farms were being constructed.

The thought of the difference his wealth could make in the world filled Eli with joy. *Perhaps getting sick was a blessing in disguise*, he thought. He was unsure when he would otherwise have had the time to dedicate to this new foray into cryptocurrencies.

He reminded himself that he should prioritize making more money, however, since reaching a net worth of $40 billion was part of his sacred obligation from his previous life—although the idea still sounded strange to Eli. By the end of those two weeks, he had reached $20 billion. *I'm halfway there*, he thought. *But what happens when I reach it?* He wondered. The question occasionally arose but never occupied much of his time or thoughts. He was more concerned about something else.

While Eli was delving into Bitcoin mining, a private investigation was underway. He had hired a detective immediately upon his return home to uncover what he could about if, or why, someone would have poisoned him. He wanted to know who was behind the phone call he had received, and the article in the newspaper about his having reported a sex trafficking ring. *Are all of these things related?* He wondered. He needed to get to the bottom of it.

He'd avoided paying any attention to the media since

his return, but Ron had informed him that a picture of him passed out at Burning Man had made its way into every major television and print entity. Headlines told fabricated stories of everything from having drug overdosed to having suffered from heat exhaustion. *What does it matter, anyway?* he thought. *Let them believe what they want to believe.*

He preferred to focus on the present. Things were much better between him and Angelina since their open conversation after his hospital stay. She had resumed her busy filming schedule, but he no longer allowed toxic thoughts and insecurities to erode their relationship. In just a couple of days, he would be going back on tour himself.

Angelina had surprised him with the idea of joining him for his first show back on the road. It would be in Phoenix—just over an hour away by plane. She'd only need to miss half a day on the set, and the director agreed to her request.

"Ready to raise consciousness?" Eli said with a wink, as they stood backstage together before the show. Angelina returned his smile. "It does feel good to be going back out there," she admitted. They'd agreed to have Angelina perform her own set as a second opening act that night. She had only five songs in her repertoire, so Eli suggested she play four of them. "That way, you'll have one more song you can play for your encore," he grinned.

"Encore? You're rather overconfident in my skills, wouldn't you say?"

"You've seen how the audience loves you. I know they'll want more." He wrapped his arms around her waist and kissed her neck. "How could anyone resist you?"

The last few notes of the first opening band were played, to which the audience cheered but not overenthusiastically.

"I'm suddenly nervous," Angelina bit her lip.

"You've got this," he gently guided her to the curtain with his hand on the small of her back. "Break a leg—isn't that what they say in film?" he smiled.

Angelina merely had to take two steps out on stage before the audience erupted in applause. Her harmonium had already been placed out front, with a microphone and a comfortable cushion. She opened with a cover song—one she'd grown up hearing at the ashram—and continued to play a few new songs she'd written before her acting schedule had gotten so hectic. Every song she sang was met with audience exhilaration. She could move them from laughter to tears and back again within the scope of a few notes.

As Eli predicted, she received an encore. Per his suggestion, she'd saved "Waterways" as her final song. By the time she made her way offstage with a giant smile, the audience was primed for a peak experience.

That's when Eli took the stage. His presence was received with intense fervor; he could see an opening in their faces—in their hearts. He knew how to help them bring that feeling home. *Get ready for the journey*, he thought. He launched into a particular pattern of notes, instrumentation, and vocal tension, the latter of which he'd systematically release, creating a simultaneous release of emotion in his audience.

During his own encore performance of the night, Eli performed an acoustic set. He called Angelina out to sing harmony. Their chemistry was magical. The audience adored them both—separately, and together.

Neither of them had been aware of Ron's presence in the shadows all night, until a young woman approached the stage and reached out to Eli, extending an envelope. Eli saw Ron move toward her with a sense of urgency, but Eli motioned him away. He could feel how her energy was not ill-intentioned.

During a break in the song's vocals, he reached out and took what he assumed was a letter. She nodded at him with tears in her eyes, holding his gaze. He could feel her gratitude. He slipped the letter into his back pocket and finished the song. He would read it later. The woman had already disappeared back into the audience.

At the end of the song, he and Angelina made their way backstage, where Eli was quickly approached by Ron.

"Before you open that envelope, may I vet it?"

"Yes, sure, if you want to. Are you concerned about something?" Eli asked.

"Just want to make sure it's only a letter."

"What else could it be?" Eli's naivete showed in his question.

"I want to check it for substances—powders such as anthrax, for example."

"Geez, really?"

"It's just a precaution. The team is a bit on edge with you back on tour. We heard back from the private investigator on your case tonight."

"And…?"

"We can go over the results in detail at your home."

"Why not here?"

"We never know when someone could be listening. Let's wait. Eric is at your home now, and the property has been on thorough surveillance."

"Fair enough. okay, let's wrap things up here and get back on the plane." Eli handed the envelope over to Ron and interrupted a conversation Angelina was in with his manager. "Ready to go home?"

She yawned. "I am."

A ONE-HOUR FLIGHT and short car ride brought Eli and Angelina home from Phoenix. Ron joined the couple at the dining room table, with a file folder before him.

"I know it's late," he began. "Are you sure you want to go through this tonight?"

"Absolutely," Eli answered.

"I'd like to know what's going on, too," Angelina added.

"Alright, then let's get started. The team has uncovered quite a bit. To begin with, we now know who made the warning phone call you received."

"Seriously? Who?"

"Let me start at the beginning. You made a phone call to the sex trafficking hotline back in January."

"Yes…"

"A staff member—who no longer works for the hotline—recognized your voice and attempted to profit from that knowledge. He called major media publications up and down the east and west coasts, but none of them considered the source credible; he had no proof. The only one that would buy his tip was the entertainment newspaper, which published the article you read. As you know, however, the publication is known for its lack of reputability and is largely written off by the general public and other media outlets as bogus. However…"

Eli and Angelina stayed quiet, in anticipation.

"The Grand Palace Hotel in Bangkok got wind of the article. You two were right. It turns out, one of the world's largest sex trafficking rings had been operating there for years…decades, even."

"Holy crap…" Eli muttered under his breath.

"The hotel owner freaked out. Even though he knew this particular paper didn't hold much merit, he knew it was just a matter of time before the story was further investigated and resurrected—no doubt, by a powerful media outlet. If, or rather when, that happened, his five-star hotel would be under heavy legal scrutiny, bombarded with negative media coverage, and inevitably shut down. So…he made a deal."

"With who?" Eli asked.

"Government and law enforcement entities, from several countries."

"What kind of deal?"

"That he would turn over all of the names involved in the ring in exchange for zero media coverage about their involvement, plus a security detail to protect himself."

"So, what happened?"

"Law enforcement investigated the hotel's claims and they turned out to be authentic. The ringleaders have been put in jail, and the ring has been officially closed down."

"Oh my god…" Eli would have felt proud that all of that had transpired due to his having made that phone call, but he couldn't help but feel sad for all of the girls who had been abused over so many years.

"What happened to the girls?" Angelina asked.

"That's not in the report," Ron admitted.

"They will need support…years of therapy…" tears formed in Angelina's eyes.

"So wait, who made the phone call to my house?" Eli was trying to put all of the pieces together.

"A former police officer. His name cannot be released, for his own safety. But let's just say he's a fan of yours. He wanted to protect you from what he'd become privy to. As the Bangkok hotel story unfolded, the U.S. government naturally investigated you—after all, your name was listed in the newspaper article."

"The U.S. government has been watching me?" Eli asked, dumbfounded.

"Of course. It's only natural—someone with your level of fame always has a file. Yours has simply grown as of late."

"So…what does the government care about me? I've done nothing of interest to them."

"Actually, you have." Ron gave a sideways glance toward Angelina. "Are you sure you want all of the details tonight? We can continue this tomorrow."

"Ron, just tell me. Tell us."

"Okay. Government officials started paying more attention to your music—" Ron turned toward Angelina, "—and your music. They've been to every one of your shows over the past year," he turned back toward Eli.

"Shit…" Eli was in awe.

"They began to understand the scope of what you were doing. Your music is in conflict with the government's goals."

"What do you mean?"

"I mean…these officials became aware of the power of your music to spark a revolution that was contradictory to the U.S. government's desire to expand the military and establish a new world order. Your music inspires peace—not the angst necessary to initiate chaos and pit man against man, country against country. How could the government successfully recruit for the military, if the people no longer feel anger or a need for revenge?" Ron asked. "You have simply become too popular, too famous, and too influential for the government to ignore."

"So, what does all of this mean?"

"It means, there might be people trying to kill you."

Angelina gasped. Eli's mouth dropped open as things began to get clearer. "The belladonna then…someone was actually trying to kill me?"

"It's quite possible."

"Who? Who the fuck was it?"

"Likely a scapegoat hired by the government to do their dirty work."

"Jesus…" Eli swallowed. "So, who is the guy that poisoned me? Tell me."

Ron pulled a photo out of the file and slid it over to him.

It was one of the many photos that had circulated throughout the media after his collapse at Burning Man. This one was taken as he was being ushered out of an ambulance and into the hospital in Reno. Standing in the background, now circled in red, was a man in dreadlocks Eli immediately recognized. The man's face wore an obvious smirk.

"Look familiar?" Ron asked.

"Yes. He's the one that gave me the iced tea earlier that day. How did he get to the hospital so fast? I came by helicopter before getting into the ambulance."

"The government has private planes too, you know."

Eli nodded, "I see."

"By the way, it turns out you had wandered off festival grounds when you encountered him."

"Huh? How do you know?"

"The festival released a private report that one of their staff members, who was monitoring the perimeter of the grounds, was drugged and later found, conscious, near the location where you described meeting this man. The man you met was not part of the festival. We know who he is and where he lives. But we can't turn him into law enforcement officials because they—or the government that they report to—are involved in the whole scheme."

"So how can these government agents—and whoever works for them—be stopped?" Angelina asked.

"We're still trying to figure that out," Ron answered, apologetically.

Neither Eli nor Angelina slept much that night. Despite exhaustion, Angelina returned to the set the following day, once again accompanied by Eric. She was grateful that at least work would help get her mind off of what felt out of her control. *Talk about a practice in faith.* She reflected upon how her spiritual beliefs encourage surrender—and emphasize that everything that happens in life is for our greater good. *Something good must come out of this.*

Ron had stayed on the property overnight, and Eli invited him to join him in the kitchen for breakfast. Eli made juice for himself and eggs and toast for Ron. He had rehearsals later that afternoon but was intent on relaxing during the early part of the day, so he could absorb all of the information from the night before.

"How was the night?" Eli asked, sleepily.

"Fine. Nothing to note. Oh—I almost forgot," Ron pulled out the envelope the fan had given to him on stage the night before. "It's clear."

"Thank you." Eli took the envelope, which had now been opened, and reached in and pulled out a letter. He unfolded it and read it to himself:

Dear Eli,

I hope this letter gets to you. I admire the work you're doing in the world, especially the benefit concerts you hold for victims of human trafficking. I was almost a victim myself.

There's something that happens all too often that I think you should know about. It's something that has happened even right in front of your nose. This is not the first time I've seen you in person—and I don't mean at one of your concerts.

I saw you in Milan, Italy once. It was at a major party. Guests in attendance included celebrities such as yourself, major film producers, and famous clothing line representatives. I was hired to be there. I am a model, and the party's organizers wanted to offer "eye candy" for the evening's guests.

I took the job because I thought it would a good opportunity to network. Sure enough, a representative from one of the world's leading clothing lines (I won't say which one, in order to protect myself) approached me early on in the night. He invited me to go to Bali with him to do a photo shoot—for a substantial amount of money. I was flattered, but something didn't sit well with me. He asked me for my passport number, which I've been told by other girls never to give. I told him I needed time to talk to my agent, but he insisted I needed to give him an answer that night.

I attempted to call the agency that represents me, but it was after hours and no one answered. I was torn. It seemed like a major opportunity. But in the end, I trusted my instincts and I told him I could not give him an answer that night, so he withdrew the offer.

The next day, I told my agent about it. She said all of the signs were there for it having been a sex trafficking scheme. Other girls have fallen for it. They are given an offer they can't refuse, and while en route to "Bali," they are kidnapped and sold into trafficking.

So you see, one of those girls you help raise money for could easily have been me. Every day, I say gratitude that was not my fate. I appreciate what you do—but I want to encourage you to consider that it's not enough. The problem is way bigger than anyone from the general public believes or that anyone from the government will admit. In fact, members at the highest level of government are participants themselves. As are many celebrities, probably many that you rub shoulders with.

Again, thank you for what you are already doing. But if you understood the depth of the problem, I think you would want to do more.

Yours truly,
Monique

"Wow…" Eli said aloud. "Did you read this?"

"I did. I wanted to make sure it wasn't a threat."

Eli re-folded the letter and tucked it into his shirt pocket. He would make a point to talk to Angelina about it the next moment they had alone together.

"Excuse me, Ron. I'm going to go into the studio for a bit and work on some new material."

"Go for it. I'll be standing guard," Ron nodded.

Eli retreated to the basement; he'd had a small home studio installed before they'd moved in. Angelina called it his man cave.

He spent the next several minutes in a comfortable

corner chair, an acoustic guitar leaning across his knees. He wasn't focused on playing it, but his fingers naturally strummed the nylon strings in a sort of meditation. Keeping his hands busy helped him think.

The letter had affected him, but more on his mind at that moment were the things the private investigator had uncovered. He had received several death threats throughout his career but knowing that members at the highest level of government were behind an actual attempt to take his life filled him with anxiety.

Maybe I should reach out to Michael, he thought. *It has been a while since we've talked, and I could sure use some guidance now.*

As always, the thought alone summoned Michael to the room.

"Howdy, Stranger." Michael grinned, now seated in the chair across from him.

"Hey, Michael."

"Heavy stuff happening, isn't there?"

"You can say that again. You know all about the attempt on my life then?"

"Of course."

"It's absurd to think that the U.S. government is after *me*. I mean, I knew the government was corrupt, but seriously? A death warrant on someone because he's making *music*?"

"It's very powerful music, Eli."

"Even so…it's hard to believe."

"In any case, it's probable that this is not all just about your music, either. You are participating in other practices that give the government great cause for concern."

"The crypto stuff, right?" The thought had already occurred to Eli.

Michael didn't answer verbally, but his eyes affirmed his suspicion.

"But what concerns me is...how can their intentions be stopped? It's not just one person or even a number of people...it's leaders of a country!"

"A tough task, indeed."

"Michael, you're not helping."

"Give me a minute...I'm thinking."

"I thought you already had all the answers."

"Even guides need time to consider what is best in certain situations."

"Speaking of which, didn´t you tell me I wouldn´t need security at Burning Man? And that I wouldn´t be recognized? Clearly, you were wrong."

"That is true. But there was a purpose behind those statements. Trust me. Now, avllow me some time to think..."

"Okay." Eli left Michael a period of silence. Michael stood from his chair and began pacing back and forth, his hands clasped together and his forefingers tapping his mouth.

"I have an idea." Michael's face lit up as he abruptly stood still.

"I'm listening..."

"What we need to do is raise the consciousness of the powers that be in the government—the very thing they are fighting against." He paused before continuing. "But...it's very difficult to change deeply ingrained beliefs and fears."

"So, what's your idea?"

"What sometimes works in these situations is for such individuals to have spiritual experiences of their own. But of course, these types of people are likely to deny the existence of a spiritual realm, even in the face of those experiences. What they are more willing to consider and accept, however, is social proof."

"Social proof?"

"Validation from others whose opinions they admire. Humans are easily swayed by their peers—especially ones in positions of high power."

"I don't see where you're going with this."

"Do you remember the sacred contract you signed?"

"Yes, you remind me of it regularly…"

"Then do you remember that the contract is upheld through a membership organization named Gemini?"

"I remember you saying something about Gemini."

"Good. Well, the organization is made up of high-powered elites. Very wealthy men and women who have been invited into its inner circle. They are individuals who aren't necessarily living current lives of integrity, who tend to be ruled by greed and fear. Men such as yourself, in your previous life."

"Fair enough."

"I have a feeling that if the government officials who are orchestrating this crime against you were invited into Gemini—using the same methods you were swayed by as Derek Stryker—they might come to have a change of heart. Or rather, a change in mind. Karma can be a bitch," Michael winked.

"I want to make sure I understand what you're saying. Essentially, this Gemini group would inform these men of the existence of an afterlife?"

"An afterlife, somewhat, but more so the reality of their future lives. If they are brought under the wing of this organization, they will discover the existence of the karmic nature of life—and the fact that nothing they do is unseen. That fear alone may be enough to alter their current behavior."

"But how would they be convinced to join?"

"The same way you were—by making them feel special. Massaging their egos a bit. Showing them file after file of well-known, wealthy, and respected names who have joined before them. They would then be encouraged to sign a sacred contract—the same as you, or Derek Stryker, signed—that guarantees them wealth and prestige in the next life. It's an offer few can refuse."

"Brilliant."

"Thank you, thank you," Michael smiled.

"But, how do I get in touch with these Gemini people?"

"Incidentally, the organization is based right here in Los Angeles. Many of your peers are also members. Most people simply don't talk about it publicly."

"Interesting."

"Ask around. Then reach out to some of the wealthiest individuals you know. Ask them if they've heard of Gemini. And don't be surprised if they are members. If they act confused, just change the subject. If they look at you knowingly, ask them how you might get in touch with the elders. Members are eager to connect others to the organization, so long as you meet certain criteria. And believe me, you do."

Michael held Eli's gaze until he was certain Eli would take action in response to his guidance.

"And might I suggest, in response to the letter you received from your fan, that many of these men after your life are the same ones participating in the sex trafficking rings she alludes to. The benefits of reaching them would be twofold."

Michael crossed over toward the back of the studio. "I believe I've given you enough food for thought for one day. Until next time, my friend." He winked and departed, morphing into the studio's rear wall.

CHAPTER EIGHT

⋯⋯⋙⟨⟩⋘⋯⋯

GEMINI

It didn't take long for Eli to discover more information about Gemini. He had a show the next night in Las Vegas, which was followed by a VIP cocktail party at Jewel Nightclub, located within the Aria Hotel and Casino. He hadn't been privy to the guest list—often, he had no idea who would be invited to his own parties—but his PR manager made certain industry elites were always present.

A gentleman in a suit, standing at the bar, caught his attention. Tucked in the man's chest pocket was what Eli knew to be a limited-edition Boehme Papillion fountain pen by Montblanc. Encrusted in diamonds and sapphires and worth upwards of $200,000, the pen represented prestige—and probably ego. He suspected the man may know a thing or two about Gemini.

"Good evening," Eli approached the gentleman.

"Mr. Evans. It's a pleasure," the man extended his hand out to Eli. "Great show tonight."

"Thank you," Eli nodded. "I don't believe we've met?"

"Not officially. Marc Germaine. Global Elite Finances."

Eli recognized the name. Marc was head of the international investment group. The type of man he usually avoided.

"Nice to meet you," he responded warmly. "What brings you here?"

"Well, you, frankly. Your PR person sent me an invitation to your show and this party. I was already in town for a meeting and figured it sounded like an enjoyable way to spend an evening. And it was."

"Happy to hear it. Do you attend a lot of these types of events?" Eli wasn't sure how to go about questioning him about Gemini.

"I do. The best business deals evolve out of events like this."

"I can see that. You seem to be doing quite well in business. I noticed your pen."

The man grinned. "Ah, yes. This baby. She's one of several that I own. I like to have options. You know how it is with beautiful women." The man winked, which made Eli feel rather disgusted.

"What do you do with all that money?"

"What do you do with yours?" Marc smiled. "You can never have too much, in my opinion."

Eli saw an opportunity. "What about after we die? It's a pity to have it go to waste, don't you think?"

"Ah, yes, it would be. Thankfully, I don't have to worry about that," the man looked to Eli with imploring eyes. He was trying to get a gauge on Eli, just as Eli was trying to get a gauge on him.

"Have you...made arrangements with a...charity of sorts?" Eli asked.

"Yes, the Marc Germaine charity," Marc laughed. "I've left it to myself." He leaned in closer to Eli. "Do you believe in reincarnation?"

"I do."

"Good for you. I didn't before. But a fine group of gentlemen helped me see the light. I could arrange a meeting with them for you if you'd like. I imagine you've acquired quite a bit of wealth yourself that would be disappointing to lose."

"I'd like that very much." *This was too easy*, Eli thought.

Marc reached into his jacket pocket and pulled out a card from a 24-karat gold business card holder. "Give this number a call. Tell them Marc Germaine sent you. They will be very pleased to meet you."

Eli took the card from Marc. There was no writing on the card, other than a phone number and what Eli recognized as the astrological symbol for Gemini. On the back of the card was the Star of David. "Thank you. I appreciate it," he extended his hand out to Marc. "Enjoy the party," Eli nodded and made his way through the party and upstairs to his penthouse suite.

Even though it was past 2 a.m., Eli wasted no time in calling the number on the card. *If no one answers, I'll try tomorrow*, he considered.

He took a deep breath and dialed the number. It only rang once before a deep, male voice answered.

"Eli. We've waited a lifetime to hear from you."

"Umm…how did you know who was calling?" Eli was already caught off guard, not only by the fact that the man knew who he was but by his choice of words. *Waited a lifetime?*

"We make it our business to know everything about everyone who is anyone."

"I see…" Eli shrugged. *Not only do I have the media and the U.S. government watching my every move, I have some secret society up in my business,* too, he thought.

"But in addition, Marc Germaine notified us that you were likely to call."

That was fast, Eli thought. "Listen, I've got a bit of a situation."

"Yes, indeed you do. The government wants to kill you, do they not?"

Eli was surprised once again by the man's bluntness.

"It seems that way."

"It's true, it does. But let's not discuss it now. In two days' time, you have a scheduled day off."

"That's true, I do…"

"Yes. I will be ready to welcome you. Tomorrow, you will receive an invitation through your assistant to a party later in the month. Ignore the date—simply show up to the address on the invitation this Sunday."

"Okay…"

"It will be *so* good to see you, Eli."

"You too." *I guess,* Eli added silently, still not sure of who this man actually was.

TRUE TO THE MAN's word, an invitation arrived via Eli's assistant the following day. He folded the piece of paper and placed it inside his wallet. He had a show that night in Bakersfield, after which he'd return home for a day of rest.

After arriving home late that night, he debated whether or not to tell Angelina where he would be going during his day off—a day he typically tried to reserve for time with her. He admitted the whole idea sounded absurd. *I'm meeting with a secret society to determine if they can get govern-*

ment officials to believe in karma and sign sacred contracts and therefore lose interest in taking my life. However, he thought it might ease some of her anxiety to know something was being done about his precarious situation.

It turns out, he had underestimated her understanding. She already knew about Gemini; she'd met her fair share of film industry elites who had covertly talked about the organization at various events.

"That sounds like it's worth a try," she shared. "I know the organization is led by very powerful people. Perhaps they will have an influence on these men. Do you want me to come with you?"

"I think it's best if I go on my own," he'd answered, still unsure what he was really getting himself into. "I will go first thing in the morning. I should be home by dinner to tell you all about it," he kissed her forehead as they settled into bed.

Eli awoke the next morning feeling somewhat anxious. He chose to drive himself to the meeting. He could have asked Ron to accompany him, but he had the sense he should go alone. *Besides, how would I explain this to Ron?* he thought.

A forty-five-minute drive from his home in Carbon Beach then through hills and forests on the outskirts of Los Angeles led him to a dead-end driveway with an elaborate iron gate. The security guard must have recognized who he was and been expecting him because he greeted Eli by name and opened the gate. Driving further up the driveway, he was in awe of the palatial property before him.

The landscaping was impeccable; a feast for his senses surrounded him. Exotic trees and flowers painted the grounds with an array of color. Water features were every which way he looked. He even noticed saltwater tidepools, bursting with brightly colored sea stars and anemone.

Finally, he reached a roundabout and the entrance to the main building on site. An elderly man in a suit stood ready to welcome him. Eli pulled over, parked and exited his vehicle.

"Mr. Evans, such a delight," the gentleman stepped forward with his hand extended. Eli greeted him and returned his handshake. The man did not share his name. "When you've lived as long as I have, you lose track of your own name after a while," the man said. "Come, come. Let me show you to the library."

Eli followed the man through a grand hallway and into a large meeting room. *This feels eerily familiar*, he thought. The room had marble floors, vaulted ceilings, and hand-crafted wooden shelves lined with hundreds of antique books. Spanish fresco paintings decorated the walls.

"Please, have a seat." Eli was directed to the mahogany conference table in the middle of the room. "Now, how do you feel we can be of service to you?"

"Well, it sounds like you are aware of my situation. I was hoping…you might be able to apply some of your influence to persuade the government members who are trying to take my life to not do so."

"Indeed."

Eli continued, "I understand you have a successful track record of turning non-believers onto the concept of karma."

"That we do."

"My thinking is that if they believe they will suffer in the next life—and lose all the wealth they have accumulated in this life—they would not want to cause harm to me or to others in this life."

"True. It is more or less that simple. The process also requires them to sign a sacred contract. Perhaps you've heard of the document?"

"Yes, a thing or two. I understand that I signed it in my previous life."

"You did. Right in this very room, in fact." Chills suddenly ran down Eli's spine as his eyes wandered around the room once again. *This is wild*, he thought. *I have been here before.*

"Would you like to see it?"

Eli brought his attention back to the man. "I...I guess so."

The man stood slowly, bracing himself against the table for support. "My knees are not as good as they were when we met last," he winked. He went over to the wall and pushed a button that was hidden behind a book. Suddenly, the bookshelf rotated, revealing an opening to a long hallway.

Lining the hallway were wooden file cabinets, labeled according to the alphabet. He went over to the drawer marked "St" and pulled out a leather-bound file folder. "Here we are. Stryker." The man extended the folder out to Eli.

Eli lightly ran his fingers over the folder before opening it slowly. The contract laid out the terms of Derek Stryker's commitment—the value of his assets that would be entrusted to Gemini, and the amount designated to his family upon his death. His eyes glazed over the details before landing sharply upon Derek's signature. *Ohmygod.* Eli thought. *That is my handwriting.*

"Funny, isn't it?" the man asked.

"Hmm?"

"So many people think they cease to exist after death.

But there's always another life ahead. And the similarities across their many lives are uncanny, really. Most people make the same choices."

The man continued, "Do you know how I know these men attempting to take your life will be unsuccessful, Eli?"

"How?"

"Because your contract has not been fulfilled. Your net worth has not yet reached $40 billion. You have work still to do on this planet. Therefore, you need not worry yourself. We will take care of your situation."

"So, you will meet with the men orchestrating the attempts on my life?"

"Of course. They were on our radar even before your call. We have men in the field, primed to intercept any future attempt, and likewise to receive prestigious invitations to our headquarters here. Once we meet with them, they will be hard-pressed to decline our offer. Very few ever have."

"Wow. Thank you."

"No 'thank you' is necessary. We are just doing our job. Speaking of which…have you given thought to signing another contract yourself?"

Eli was taken aback at the suggestion. "I don't know… to be honest I never thought about it."

"Understandable. You are young. You are still living out your last contract. But it's worth considering. You know, you have signed the contract in your previous forty-two lives."

"*Forty-two* lives?!"

"Oh, yes. You have been a wealthy man for many, many generations, my friend. Would you like to see them?"

"Wait…see what?"

"Your previous lives. You can see all of them, in fact— even the ones before you were involved in Gemini. Once someone becomes a member, we gain access to that individual's entire history. Come, I will take you to our past life chamber. There is a comfortable screening room there."

Eli didn't move with the man, so he continued, "Don't worry, it doesn't take long. You receive the information as a download of sorts. You will experience each life in a matter of seconds."

Eli's curiosity got the best of him. He followed the man back through the library, down a narrow hallway, and into what felt like a small movie theater.

"On the screen, you will see a series of very fast images, beginning with your very first life and working up to the current day. The information you receive, however, will be more acutely integrated by what you feel, rather than what you see. Along with each image, you will experience sensations—emotions, fears, smells, and so forth—that help you understand what you lived through. Are you ready to begin?"

"I suppose so," Eli took a seat in a reclining chair.

"Good. I will leave you some privacy. I will be waiting for you in the library when you are ready."

As soon as the door shut, the room became pitch dark. Just as he was beginning to wonder why nothing was happening, an image of a night sky appeared. From a shooting star, he watched—and felt—the birth of himself as a small insect. His first lifetime was remarkably short, but not void of sensations. He experienced fear when he became caught in a spider's web and subsequently died. From there, his lifetimes progressed to larger and more sentient beings—he was a squirrel, a rabbit, a kangaroo, a dinosaur. His first human life was as a young boy in Africa.

Every sensation and emotion that there was to feel, he

Petra Nicoll

felt—hunger, joy, abandonment, unconditional love. He was not always a human thereafter; sometimes he reverted to being in animal form—such as an elephant or a whale. His human lives were extremely diverse; he was an Egyptian princess, a Viking warrior, a dictator, a peasant. He died from murder, starvation, suicide, disease. All of the lives intrigued him, but one, in particular, stood out.

Several lifetimes before, prior to ever having joined Gemini, he was a dolphin. The sensations he experienced as such were unlike any other. He felt connected to the highest level of frequency available on the planet. He felt an innate sense of knowing; a wisdom and understanding of the world that humans most often never reach.

Interestingly, whereas some humans do reach what is called enlightenment, he considered, *every single dolphin* he encountered was enlightened. They lived in ecstasy; complete joy, love, and transparency. They were playful, non-competitive, and non-judgmental. They were teachers, he felt—brought to earth to help lead humans to a higher consciousness.

Eli was blown away by the experience. It lasted all too quickly, however. He returned to human form in the next life. *Why would I ever have left that feeling?!* He wondered. But as soon as he posed the question, he received an answer. *To lead humans to a higher realm of consciousness in a form they understand.*

As he watched his most recent lives unfold, he also understood that he had deliberately chosen to be human again in order to remember what it was like to be human. This way, he could better relate to those he was trying to serve. With that recent experience in his memory (whether consciously or unconsciously), he could share the frequency he'd lived among as a dolphin with humans. In his current life, he did this through music. Eli acknowledged with gratitude that, within the limitations of being human, he'd discovered and begun to achieve what he'd set out to do in this life.

He knew he'd only hit the tip of the iceberg in regard to the number of people he was meant to reach with this music, but he knew he was on the right path. *It only takes ten percent of a population to start a revolution,* he thought. He could get there in this lifetime. And once he did, he wanted to return to being a dolphin. He was certain about that.

The following lives that he witnessed were dull, at best. Although sometimes male and sometimes female, he was always wealthy and often egotistical. He was proud, however, of the growth he witnessed in himself in his current life. *I've come a long way since Derek Stryker,* he thought. He understood, as well, that Derek's life had served him well. *No life is ever wasted,* he considered.

As he exited the screening room he made his way to the library with conviction and confidence.

"Welcome back. How was that experience for you?" the man asked.

"Powerful. Incredible. Thank you for that opportunity."

"Our pleasure. Now, have a seat. Let's discuss the opportunity to sign another contract with Gemini, shall we?"

"With all due respect, there is no need to discuss anything. I am certain of my decision."

"Is that so? And what is your decision?"

"The contract…it only applies to human lives."

"How do you figure?"

"Humans are the only species that believe in monetary values. We experience greed, desire, and attachment like no other beings."

"This is true. Well done."

"So, by signing that contract, an individual is essentially trapping himself into the karmic responsibility of returning to life in human form."

"Go on…"

"I do not wish to return to life in human form. I want to return as a dolphin. I was a dolphin in a past life, and I experienced the highest form of consciousness that exists on this planet. I believe I can continue to be of service to humanity in that form."

"If that is your choice, I will not try to persuade you differently. But…"

"Yes?"

"There is still more for you to do in this life. More money for you to earn. And more for you to learn."

Eli nodded.

"We will make sure nothing gets in your way," the man rested his hand on Eli's shoulder.

"Thank you." Eli shook the man's hand and made his way back out to his car.

CHAPTER NINE

───∞∞∞───

NEWS FROM BROWNSVILLE

It was late evening when Eli returned home after his visit to Gemini. He had two things he immediately wanted to share with Angelina—the contents of the letter he'd received from his fan, and his experience at Gemini. Fortunately, Angelina was already home and had prepared a nice vegetarian meal in anticipation of the news Eli would have to share. It was a treat when either of them had time to cook and eat a meal together, and they both savored it.

"Well, how was it?" Angelina asked after the two of them said gratitude and began their meal.

"It was…pretty incredible," Eli answered.

"Are they going to try to talk to the people who want to take your life?"

"Yes, yes. They assured me it would be taken care of and that I don't need to worry about that anymore."

"I certainly hope that's the case…"

"It is. I am sure of it, Ang. I believe them. Actually, I learned something important while I was there."

"That's good to hear. What did you discover?"

"I got to see each of my past lives…"

"Wow. I've never been quite sure if that's a good thing or not…"

"For me, it was."

"What did you see?"

"It's more about what I felt. I felt what it's like to be a dolphin."

"A dolphin?"

"Yes. I was a dolphin in a past life. I don't even know if I can describe what it was like in words…it was so powerful. Dolphins are incredibly empathetic and altruistic, not individualistic like us. They feel and express love like I never imagined to be possible…and in turn, they experience profound joy."

"Yes, I know that about dolphins. I could feel it when I swam with them."

"You swam with dolphins?"

"Yes. In the wild, not ones in captivity. In captivity, their essence has been stripped away from them and they're deeply depressed. They're forced to interact with humans in order to be fed. But in the wild, they often seek out opportunities to engage with humans out of curiosity and play. That's what happened to me; I was snorkeling in Hawaii when a pod of bottlenose dolphins came to check me out. I was eye-to-eye with one; I felt it could see into my soul. I felt so much love at that moment."

"Yes! So, you get it?"

"Absolutely. I think there's a lot we can learn from them."

"Exactly! That's what I came to conclude. It's why…" Eli caught himself, realizing he hadn't told Angelina yet about Michael or the sacred contract he had signed in his previous lives.

"Yes?"

"It's complicated. There's something I haven't told you."

"You can tell me."

"I know…it just sounds crazy."

"I already think you're crazy," Angelina winked.

Eli relaxed a bit at her gesture. "I was a member of Gemini in my last life."

"Really? Fascinating. Did you find that out during your meeting?"

"Yes. But I knew it before the meeting, too."

"You did? How?"

"Through…my guide. Michael."

"Michael?"

"Yes. I…I've been meeting with him for several years now."

"Ah, the elusive spiritual teacher you've mentioned?"

"Yes. But he's not…human. He's actually a spirit."

Angelina was quiet for a moment—long enough for Eli to wonder if he should regret what he'd just shared.

Finally, she answered, "I suspected as much."

"Wait, you did?" *How does she know so much?* Eli wondered.

"Yes. I hear you talking sometimes when there's no one else around."

"Really?"

"Yeah…like the time we were visiting your parents. Did you really think I believed you were talking to your dad in the middle of the night? I know he sleeps like a log." She smiled.

"Why didn't you say something?"

"Why didn't *you*?"

"I don't know. Maybe I liked having a secret. More likely, I didn't think you'd understand. But you always surprise me."

"Did it ever occur to you that I have a spiritual guide, too?"

Eli's blank expression clearly communicated that he had not. "Seriously?"

"Yes, seriously," she laughed.

"Why didn't you tell me?"

"Maybe I liked having a secret," Angelina answered playfully. "More likely, the right moment never seemed to arrive. But now it has," she added.

"Fair enough."

"So, what were you going to tell me? About what you concluded after your dolphin experience?"

"Well, Gemini asked me to sign another contract for my next life. To earn back the money I made in this life."

"What did you say?"

"I said no. I realized that if I did, I would be guaranteed to reincarnate in human form."

"That's a wise assumption. I have a feeling many people don't consider that there are other options."

"And I don't want to be a human. I want to be a dolphin again."

"That's beautiful, Eli."

"I can't believe you don't think I'm crazy. Like, for real."

"Of course not. You've always known I believe in reincarnation."

"I know. Anyway, I was rested assured I have a lot left to do yet in this life." Eli remembered the second thing he wanted to share with Angelina.

"There's something else I wanted to talk with you about tonight," he said, between bites.

"Go ahead."

"Ron shared the letter from the fan with me."

"That you were handed onstage the other night?"

"Yes."

"What did it say?"

Eli pulled it out of his wallet and handed it to Angelina.

She read it quietly. "Wow," she said after she was through. "That's heavy."

"Yeah, I know."

"What are you going to do about it?"

"I wish I knew…"

"Maybe you can ask Michael what he thinks about that," she smiled.

"Maybe I will," he grinned back across the table. He set the idea aside for later. Tonight was to be spent exclusively with Angelina.

THE PLEASURE ELI derived from the previous night with Angelina was replaced with anxiety the following morning when he received a phone call from his mother. She rarely called outside of birthdays and holidays, so he instantly felt uneasy. His discomfort turned out not to be unfounded.

"Hello?"

"Eli? Are you sitting down?" She asked.

"Yes, Mom. What is it?" He could hear the distress in her voice, and his heart immediately started to race.

"Something happened to your father last night…"

"What? What happened? Is he okay?"

"He's okay. But he's no longer with us."

"What do you mean? Is he okay or isn't he?"

"He collapsed on his way to the bathroom last night, Eli. He had a ruptured heart aneurysm. By the time the medics got here, it was too late."

Eli had not been sitting, as he'd promised his mother, and he fell to the floor in grief.

"No...no..."

"I'm so sorry to have to share this news with you, Eli. It breaks my heart."

Carol let him sob uncontrollably for several minutes until Eli gathered himself enough to order and express some of his thoughts.

"Where is he...I mean where are you? Are you okay?"

"Yes, I am as good as can be expected, I suppose. I am at home. My parents are on their way here from Idaho, so I will not be alone. They will be helping make arrangements."

"I will come too, Mom. I will get on the plane today."

"You do not need to, Eli. I know what your schedule is like. Why don't you wait until arrangements have been made? It will be more important for you to be here for his service."

"I wouldn't dream of not coming, Mom. I have missed being with you both too much already. Now, I'm too late for Dad..." Eli couldn't hold back his tears again.

"Don't think about it that way, Son. Your father was very proud of you. He knows you did what you had to do to play music."

"Fuck music! I should have been there for you guys."

"Eli, please don't talk like that. You're not thinking straight. Honestly, I don't think it's a good idea for you to be here yet. Take a couple of days to rest at home. Spend some time with Angelina."

"Mom, I'm coming home. I will see you soon. I love you." Eli hung up the phone before she could further disagree.

He immediately called his pilot and made arrangements to fly to Eugene, Oregon in a few hours. A driver would meet him at the airport and take him the remaining half-hour to Brownsville.

Next, he called his manager. Russ was sympathetic and assured him he'd take care of re-arranging his tour schedule so that he could take the time he needed to be with his family.

The next call he made was to Angelina. She didn't answer her phone, so he called the studio and asked to speak with her.

"I'm coming home now. Wait there for me," she said urgently.

"I'm flying to Brownsville in a couple of hours."

"I'm coming with you then."

"You don't have to, love. Maybe it's better if you stay in L.A. for now. I'll let you know when the service is and you can come then so you don't miss so much time on the set."

"Eli, being together is more important. I can only imagine how you feel right now. I want to be there for you."

"I know, and I appreciate that. But…maybe it's best for me to have some alone time with my mom right now."

"Are you sure?"

"Yes, I'm sure. You can meet us there later in the week. I'll arrange things with my pilot to pick you up."

"Okay, if that's what you feel you need right now…"

To be honest, Eli wasn't sure what he needed. He felt on the verge of a breakdown, and he preferred not to have Angelina witness it.

"I think it's best. Ang, I love you."

"I love you, too. So much, Eli."

Eli hung up the phone and began packing.

His THOUGHTS TURNED toxic throughout the two-hour flight to Eugene. *Why wasn't I there more?* The question played on repeat in his head. *Why did this happen? He was still too young to die. How did I miss the signs? He seemed in great health. I wasn't paying attention. I'm a fucking terrible son...*

When he arrived at the farm, his mother was there to greet him on the porch. No words were exchanged, they simply fell into a warm embrace. Eli felt like a child, holding onto his mother for support. He knew if he let go, he wouldn't be able to stand on his own.

His grandparents had not yet arrived, so the two of them were alone. Carol guided Eli to the porch swing, and together they sat and cried. She stroked his head, brushing his hair as she did when he was a boy.

Finally, Eli broke the silence. "What's going to happen now, Mom?"

"We grieve. And then we go forward with our lives. Just as your father would have wanted."

"How can you be so calm about everything?" Eli couldn't understand why she didn't seem as devastated as he felt.

"We all leave our bodies at some point, Eli. In a way, I had our over thirty years of marriage to prepare for this moment. We talked about it often, what would happen should the other pass. We had even talked about it last week, in fact."

"Did he know he was going to die?"

"Maybe not so soon. But I do think he knew more than he let on. Something shifted in him over the past few weeks."

"It did? Why didn't you tell me? Why didn't he tell me?

I could have been here…"

"Everything happens as it's supposed to, Eli."

"I don't know about that anymore." Eli felt overwhelmed with guilt over not having spent more time with his family over the years. He'd taken them for granted, even after his time spent in the Caribbean and everything his spiritual awakening had taught him.

"I let my career control my life…"

"You have a major purpose on this planet, Eli. It has required a lot of your time and energy. You are only human, you know."

Yes, I am human. He thought. *Why am I fucking human? I don't want to be human anymore. Being human just means being in pain.* His thoughts became distorted, carrying him deeper and deeper into a depressive, confused state. *What is this all for?* Questions he'd previously felt he had the answers to resurfaced. He wanted to scream. He wanted to run away. He wanted to be alone.

"Mom, I'm going to go for a walk." He kissed her cheek as she squeezed his hand. "I'll be back soon."

"Okay, Son. I will be here. I love you."

"I love you, too."

Eli wandered off on the nearby trails he'd frequented as a child. He saw the land differently than he had before; he saw the love his father had put into it—the fences he built, the soil he aerated, the food he grew. "Why aren't you here, Dad? I miss you…I miss you so much," he spoke out loud.

Just then, he felt like he was being watched. He turned around and jumped slightly.

"Michael?"

"Hello, Eli. I know I haven't come uninvited recently, but I feel you need me now."

"I don't know what I need, Michael. I thought I had direction. I understood my purpose. Now, I feel so lost and unsure if I've lived my life correctly."

"There is no right or wrong, Eli. There is only the path you choose. If you choose with your heart and soul, you have chosen correctly."

"That's the thing though, Michael. If I had chosen with my heart, wouldn't I have been there for my family more?"

"Perhaps, perhaps not. Did the choices you made in life feel right at the moment?"

"Yes, I guess so. I mean, I felt I needed to pursue music. That I'd go crazy if I didn't."

"Then you chose 'correctly.'"

"Then why does this hurt so much?"

"It hurts to lose those we love, no matter what. Even if you'd never left Brownsville, it would hurt just as much—probably even more, because you'd not have followed your passion."

"So, what now?"

"As your mother said…take the time you need to grieve, and then move on with your life. Your father will always be with you, cheering you on as he did when he was alive."

"I just wish I could have spoken with him one more time…"

"You can always speak to your father, Eli. He will always be here to listen."

"But I want to see him again…to hear his voice. It's unfair that I didn't get to say goodbye."

"That's harder to arrange while in human form…"

"Well, I can see and hear you, can't I?"

"True. But that is because I signed on to be a guide in this life."

"Maybe my father did, too…"

"It's possible. He may not have yet decided on his next life, however. He only recently crossed over."

"How can I find out? Can you find out?"

"That is between you and your father. However…"

"Yes?"

"There may be a way to communicate with him while he's in the other realm…"

"How? Tell me!"

"I can't tell you directly…"

"Here you go again…why not?"

"I am here to guide you, Eli, not tell you what to do. You must retain free will."

"Okay, *guide* me then…" Eli said sarcastically.

"Okay. You will find some answers in Thailand."

"Thailand?"

"Yes. There are multiple places you could go, actually. But karmically, I think it would be good for you to associate the country with some positive memories…not just your experience at the Bangkok hotel."

"Okay…Do I just show up in Thailand and the answers will magically appear?"

"Things will fall into place. Just follow your intuition. In fact, I recommend taking Angelina with you. You both could use some quality time together. But of course, all of these decisions remain your own."

"I'll think about it."

"Good. I'll leave you to it then. Just remember, Eli. You're never alone. And you're always right where you're supposed to be." Eli watched Michael walk off into the fields and gradually fade into thin air.

CHAPTER TEN

———∽∾∿∾∽———

THE IBOGA EXPERIENCE

As promised, Angelina joined Eli, his mother, and their extended family in Brownsville a few days later for the memorial service. Eli's mother had given much thought to the ceremony and, in accordance with her husband's recently expressed wishes, no one wore black and the ceremony was not held at a funeral home or cemetery. Robert was to be cremated, and he did not want his body to be put on display.

Instead, they held a memorial celebration of his life, right there on the farm. Neighbors and friends of Robert's were invited to attend a potluck dinner on the land he had worked and held so dear. Lights were hung from trees around a long wooden table, and a colorful array of flowers surrounded the dining area. Attendees shared stories of Robert's generosity and loving spirit and infused humor into their recollections. Robert had told Carol that he expected there to be tears, but he wanted laughter to be more abundant.

And they did laugh. Everyone took turns sharing stories about Robert's quirks and corny jokes. Still, Eli struggled with the loss of his father more than he ever thought possible. He was frightened as to what was to become of the farm, and who would be able to take care of his mother as she also aged. He felt suddenly responsible—for her, for the farm, for the future of his family. *Dad left such huge shoes to fill,* he cried.

He became aware of just how strong his father's presence had been in his life—even from afar. *I thought he'd always be here,* Eli realized he'd been so naïve. Angelina and his mother did much to console him, but it was not enough. He felt distraught and devastated.

The day after the celebration, Eli shared his plans with his mother and Angelina to travel to Thailand. Angelina willingly agreed to go with him; filming had just wrapped on her screenplay. Now that it was in post-production, she could breathe a little easier until the publicity campaign launched. In addition to wanting to be with Eli during this critical time, she admitted she needed a vacation herself.

His mother supported the idea as well. She knew a vacation and a change of scenery would be just what he needed. Eli hired temporary laborers to manage the farm until he and his mother were in better emotional states to figure out future steps. Eli had offered to pay for hired labor on the farm many times over the years, but his parents had always insisted that they enjoyed taking care of it themselves. His mother admitted, however, that she could not do it alone.

Carol's parents would be staying with her on the farm for as long as she needed. "Don't worry about us, Son," Carol told Eli. "You two get some rest. Enjoy your time together. As you are experiencing, this life is short."

Petra Nicoll

Ron had not been as enthusiastic about his travel plans. "Thailand?!" Ron had exclaimed. "You're aware why that might not be such a good idea?"

"Yeah, I know, it seems crazy. But…I just have a feeling about it. We can go someplace very private—one of the islands. We'll avoid Bangkok." Eli realized Michael had not told him to go to Bangkok, and if questioned he would probably give him no more direction than he already had, so he would pick the location.

"Where do you have in mind?" Angelina asked him.

"The coast. You'll love it, the beaches are incredible and the limestone cliffs are spectacular. It's the perfect place to get our minds off everything and relax for a while."

Ron knew there was no point in trying to talk him out of it. He settled for being invited along as his bodyguard, "so long as "you give us some privacy," Eli requested. Angelina was simply happy to go wherever Eli went.

Eli already knew where he wanted to go. He'd stayed at the Panacea Koh Samui resort, located on an island off the northeast coast of Thailand, while on tour a few years before. He'd dreamed of returning someday, *with my soulmate,* he thought.

The private villa was located on a green and grassy hilltop overlooking the Gulf of Samui and tropical rainforests. The resort was a Zen-inspired sanctuary, and he knew Angelina would love it. He would rent the same luxury residence as before—Praana.

Arrangements were made for them to leave Los Angeles two days after their return home from Brownsville. In addition to the nearly twenty hours of travel time, Koh Samui was fourteen hours ahead of Los Angeles time. Eli, Angelina, and Ron would arrive jet lagged but decently rested, as Eli's private jet was optimized for long-term comfort. After exiting the plane and easily passing through customs, they were met by an obscure car and butler who drove them the remaining half hour from Samui Airport to Panacea.

They were met at the resort by a host who welcomed them with fragrant iced towels and a jasmine scented floral garland. The three were led along a stone walkway through a maze of exotic palms and rainforest blooms and above a lily-clad water feature. Buddha sculptures peaked out from enclaves, which made Angelina smile.

They passed a palm-reflecting infinity pool, a Muay Thai Boxing ring, and an opulent, open gathering space before arriving at Praana—a six-bedroom residence. Eli and Angelina chose one of the sea-facing suites with wraparound glass doors, and Ron settled into the bedroom furthest from their own—which felt like its own separate residence—to offer the couple some privacy. He would only join them when invited; otherwise, he would look after the property.

Each room had its own terrace and marble-clad bathroom with a terrazzo bathtub and Jacuzzi. "I think we're going to be quite comfortable here," Angelina's body had already relaxed, which Eli couldn't have been more delighted to observe. *This is just what we need*, he thought. *My body desperately needs to relax, too.*

Two massage tables had been arranged in the unit, overlooking the ocean. They were each treated to an exquisite Thai massage, which was followed by a gourmet, vegetarian feast. After the staff had excused themselves and the couple was left alone to enjoy their private pool, their senses were heightened to the extent that the slightest touch upon each other's skin sent shivers down th spines.

Petra Nicoll

It had been a long time since Eli and Angelina had practiced tantric sex. Their schedules simply hadn't allowed them to indulge in long-lasting pleasure. This time, prior to physical contact, they engaged in eye contact that lasted several minutes long. Angelina coached him on how to locate the tension in his chest and relax the muscles around his heart.

"Feel the pain and suffering you're holding there. Don't judge it, just feel it." Her mere suggestion brought tears to his eyes. He missed his father so much.

"Now feel my heart," she instructed. He placed his hand upon her heart. "What do you feel?"

Eli breathed deeply and released it. "Compassion," he answered. "Your care and concern."

"I'm glad," she smiled. They breathed deeply together, in and out, paying attention to the subtle energies and emotions residing in each body part, from the tops of their heads to the tips of their feet.

"You are not alone," Angelina whispered.

Eli let out a deep sigh.

"Come, let's lie down together," Angelina invited him to the bed, where the couple curved their bodies together, skin to skin, arms around each other. Breathing aligned, they tuned into each other's body language and became an extension of the other.

Angelina led the transition to more physical touch. She began to stroke and caress every inch of Eli's body, except his genitals. She had packed a bottle of lavender essential oil with her, and she reached for it now. After squeezing a few drops of the oil into the palm of her hands, she rubbed the oil into Eli's thighs, just above the knee. She worked his groin muscles with her hands, but she did not touch his penis.

Slowly, she traced her fingers in figure eights down his inner thighs, calves, and the arch of his foot. After massaging in between his toes, she worked her way back to the top of his body, massaging his ears with her fingertips. She lightly pressed upon his third eye and upon seeing Eli's state of total relaxation, she decided to stimulate another of his senses. She reached for a tray of fruit that lay on the nightstand and slipped a piece of mango into his mouth using her lips. Back and forth, they exchanged the sweet fruit until it had all but dissolved into their mouths.

By now, both of their bodies were brimming with erotic anticipation, but they both knew they couldn't release it just yet. They allowed themselves to cool down by taking turns moving a single ice cube along the length of their bodies. They understood that the longer they delayed climax, the more powerful it would be when released.

After sufficiently calmed, it was Angelina's turn to receive. She spread her legs open and bent her knees; Eli inserted his index and middle fingers inside of her until the tips of his fingers were pressing upward near her G-spot. He made a gentle "come-hither" motion with his fingers, caressing her sensitive internal areas. With his other wrist, he applied light pressure on her pubic area while his fingers danced upon her clitoris.

The level of passion between them was flaming hot. They held each other's gaze whenever possible to stay within the moment together. Finally, they were ready for intercourse. Angelina remained lying down, with her pelvis tilted slightly on a small pillow. Eli lifted her feet up so that they rested on his chest and her legs curled in. He admired the way her knees brushed up against her erect nipples.

Eli held her feet in place as he gently inserted himself into her moist, eager opening. The term "soulmates" took on new meaning to Eli in that moment. He literally felt his soul connect to hers. He could even *see* it—an emerald green aura extended from Angelina's body and merged with his own aura of gold. Together, they glowed.

The sounds of pleasure they made were in chorus with the cicadas and frogs in the distance, complemented by the aroma of jasmine, and in harmony with the light of the moon above them.

ELI AND ANGELINA hadn't slept so well in months. They felt perfectly relaxed and protected, away from the demands of their careers, the media, and the grief that had encompassed Eli while in Brownsville.

They were greeted in the morning by a tray table outside their door with freshly made beetroot, celery, and kiwi juice. "Ron must have tipped them off," they laughed together. An orchid rested delicately beside their glasses.

"This place is amazing," Angelina came up behind Eli and wrapped her arms around his waist. "Thank you for taking me here. This was your best idea yet," she winked. Eli turned around and took in her naked body. "*You* were my best idea yet," he kissed her neck, causing her to giggle.

Actually, technically this trip was Michael's idea, Eli considered to himself. He hadn't given any thought to Michael since boarding the plane. He was sure he'd be happy that he was living more in the present moment than he had in months, and that he was taking the time to reconnect to himself and to Angelina. Eli was pleased that he had no agenda to follow for the day. *Things will fall into place*, he remembered Michael saying.

At Angelina's suggestion, after slowly sipping their juice on the terrace, they called the concierge and had a yoga teacher come to their room for a private class. Angelina reveled in being the student, with no attention needing to be paid to determining the next pose. After class, they showered together under separate showerheads.

The rest of the afternoon was spent reading by the pool—the room held an extensive collection of spiritual literature—and sharing interpretations about what each other read. In the early evening, they decided to take a walk to nearby Fisherman's Village to enjoy the public beach.

As the couple lounged on beach chairs, Eli kept catching the eye of an elderly Thai gentleman several chairs over to his left. He felt the man watching him. *Does he recognize me?* Eli wondered. It would be an unexpected occurrence, as the man was not of the generation nor nationality that typically knew him or his music. In any case, the man held gentle eyes and there was nothing Eli found unsettling about his gaze.

"I'm going to go for a swim. Do you want to come with me?" Angelina stood and unwrapped the towel around her waist.

"No, you go ahead. I'll join up with you later," Eli smiled.

"Okay, see you soon!" She cheerfully sauntered off toward the sea. Eli couldn't help but admire her backside. *Damn, I'm a lucky guy*, he thought with a grin.

Eli glanced casually back over to his left out of curiosity. The chair the elderly man had been sitting in was empty.

"Hello." Eli jumped slightly. The man stood before him, speaking English with a strong accent.

"Oh, hello. You scared me."

"Sorry, not my intention," the man bowed.

"It's okay," Eli didn't know what to say next, and the man was making no eager attempt to continue speaking. However, the man did not move from his position and did not alter his gaze.

"Can I…help you with something?" Eli finally asked.

"Perhaps I help you," the man replied.

"Oh, I don't need anything. Thank you." *He must be on staff*, Eli realized.

"Are you sure?"

"Yes…"

"Why you come to Thailand, sir?"

"Excuse me?"

"You come here for answers, yes? I help you with that."

Eli looked around him, subconsciously searching for Michael. "Michael?" he said out loud.

"No, sir. My name Somsak. I help you with answers."

"I don't understand."

"Here my card," the man extended a business card out to him, with just his name and a picture of a plant. "When ready for answers, I be here. Good night, sir," the man bowed and strolled back to his chair.

That was weird, Eli thought. Several minutes later, Angelina returned to her chair. "Are you okay? You look a little pale," she bent down to kiss Eli's forehead.

"Yeah, I'm okay. Actually, I'm confused. Don't look now, but there's a man over there…"

"Yeah, I saw him come over to you. Is everything ok?"

"I think so. I mean, he handed me this. He said he could help me with answers."

Angelina looked down at the card. "That's the iboga plant," she said.

"Iboga plant?"

"Yeah, it's a rainforest shrub and psychedelic from Central Africa. Shamans have used the plant for thousands of years for spiritual development."

"Interesting," Eli pondered the meaning Angelina assigned to the card. "Do you think…he sells it? Or is a shaman or something?"

"He could be," Angelina glanced discreetly over at the man.

"What else do you know about this plant? Is it safe?" Eli was beginning to wonder if this man held the answers to the questions he had asked Michael about how to communicate with his father in another realm.

"Yes, if used properly. At the ashram, there were people who took it. It's non-addictive, and it only needs to be used once in order to have a profound impact."

"Do you…think we should try it?"

"I don't know. I mean, I've never thought about it before. I feel pretty content in my understanding of the world."

"I can't help but feel this is some sort of sign," Eli shared, without wanting to go into detail as to why. "I think we should look into it."

"Okay," Angelina shrugged.

BACK AT THE resort, Eli spent several hours researching the iboga plant with Angelina looking over his shoulder. She did not need to be convinced of its medicinal and spiritual properties, but Eli wanted a deeper understanding of the drug's history and uses. He learned that in recent years, it was becoming increasingly used as a tool to cure addiction and depression. He was less interested in those qualities, and more interested in what it could offer his soul. *Will it allow me to connect with my father?* He wondered.

He read: *For thousands of years, iboga has been used by ancient ancestor cults in Africa for healing and divination purposes. These cults believe in a spirit realm, where all souls reside. There, one can talk to the dead.*

"Bingo," Eli said out loud before reading on: *One can also have access to the infinite nature of the soul. Ingesting iboga's root bark grants entrance to this other realm.*

He knew he had to try this plant. But was the man he'd met trustworthy? Would it be safe to reach out to him?

He called Ron and asked him to have his team conduct a background check on the man. By the next morning, he had learned that Somsak was a well-respected shaman in the community. He did not operate a business, but rather a referral-only healing center in a private location on the island. He finally felt comfortable enough to reach out to him.

Later that evening, he and Angelina found Somsak lounging on the same beach chair he'd been on earlier.

"Friend, good to see you," Somsak motioned for Eli to have a seat beside him.

"Hi, Somsak. This is Angelina," Eli gestured toward Angelina. "And my name is Eli."

"Eli. Yes, yes. Nice meet you, Eli. Nice meet you, Angelina."

"You said you could help me with some answers…" Eli let his statement trail off.

"Answers, yes."

"Would you…work with us?"

"Yes, Sir. For seekers, I work."

"How does this…work?"

"I explain in detail. Come with me to my center, please. We walk."

Eli and Angelina followed him for what felt like several miles, walking through thick rainforest until they reached a primitive hut.

"Please, come in," Somsak welcomed them into the structure. The hut was simple but solid. The roof was woven from grasses, and the floors and walls made of bamboo and tied with rope. The base of the structure consisted of poles and beams made of hardwood. Inside, pillows were arranged comfortably in a circle. Shavings of root bark were stored in jars on a shelf in the corner, and whole sticks of the root were stacked beside the jars.

"Iboga. Master healer," Somsak began after gesturing for them to take a seat. "It shows you dark side. Your shadow. Very powerful. It rebalances your body, mind, spirit. And, it can allow you talk to dead. Depends on person and what he needs."

Eli felt himself get excited about the prospect of speaking with his father. However, he still had doubts. "Is it safe?"

"Depend. Some people use wrong. Too much, or health no good. Need strong heart, strong liver. Iboga very dangerous with certain substance, like caffeine." Somsak looked firmly at Eli, then Angelina and back. "If try, you try tomorrow. No food for eight hours before. Water okay, vegetable juice okay. Okay?"

"Okay," Eli replied, before looking at Angelina. "Do you want to try it tomorrow?"

Angelina was not as curious about the drug as Eli, but she could sense that finding out what it had to teach him was important to Eli. "If you take it, I will take it with you."

Eli smiled and turned back to Somsak. "Thank you. May we return tomorrow?"

"Yes, yes, tomorrow. I will be at beach. You find me

there, okay?"

"Okay," Eli and Angelina both nodded.

"Come, I take you back to beach now," Somsak led the way back through the forest and to Fisherman's Village. "I see you tomorrow my friends."

"Tomorrow. Thank you," Eli and Angelina nodded in response, but Somsak had already turned to head back to the forest.

ELI AND ANGELINA followed Somsak's instructions. They had vegetable juice for breakfast and drank water throughout the morning but arrived at the beach early the next afternoon on empty stomachs. They were both in excellent health and had no history of heart or liver conditions, but still, they were both nervous about how the plant would affect their bodies—and their minds. They'd read it could be extremely uncomfortable, physically and emotionally.

Somsak looked pleased to see them, but he led them back to the hut with hardly a word. When they arrived, he once again gestured for them to take a seat.

"You feel good?" he asked.

"Yes," Eli and Angelina answered.

"Feel good here?" Somsak placed his hand on his heart. Eli and Angelina understood his meaning not only to be about the condition of their hearts but the state of their intentions.

"Yes, sir."

"You be here overnight. Maybe two days. Last twenty-four to thirty-six hour."

"We understand," Eli and Angelina had prepared for an overnight stay, and had told Ron what they were doing.

"Okay. Slowly. Iboga know how much too much for

you, but it not easy," Somsak shared. "It knows what you need." Somsak offered each of them about a gram of the root bark every forty minutes until the entire dose had been administered.

Eli and Angelina had read that some people had gentle experiences with the drug, while others were pushed to the outer limits of their comfort zones. It didn't take long for either of them to enter what Somsak called an "awakened dream state," when both conscious and unconscious parts of the mind merged.

The experience was not pleasant for Eli. His heart beat rapidly amid a constant buzzing in his ears. He became nauseous and dizzy, and at one point had to use the paper bag Somsak had set beside each of them for illness. Finally, he began to have visions.

The visions continued in flashes of nanoseconds, evolving into images of Eli's own life. He witnessed his own birth and saw the joy in his parents' faces. He saw loving moments between him and his father from so long ago he could not have remembered them while conscious. He watched himself grow up on the farm, pick up a guitar for the first time, and perform on his first stage. Always, he saw pride and unconditional love in his father's face.

The speed, however, at which the visions came to him was nauseating. At the peak of this first phase of his experience, he threw up once again. Yet, he was very conscious of his own physical body and also his environment.

He could see Angelina beside him, having a very different experience than his own. The drug was having a gentle effect on her; she appeared at peace even during this intense stage. He was grateful; he did not want to see her writhe in pain as he was now.

When her eyes met his, he could see her empathy for his pain. She understood, however, that the detox he was going through was necessary and temporary. He was cleansing his body of negative emotions, such as the guilt he'd felt for not having spent more time with his father when he was alive.

The next phase of the drug's effects was introspection. Now, the user was to emotionally process all of the downloads he or she had received. At times over the next several hours, Eli felt withdrawn and on the verge of a dark, depressive state. At other times, he felt lighter—like a load of toxins and dead weight had been lifted from his body. Most of all, he just felt tired. The intake and processing of what he received left him overwhelmed and exhausted. He didn't know what he was supposed to do with those images. They just made him miss his father more.

Eli could see that Angelina was tired as well, but calm. "Are you okay?" he asked her through heavy breaths and perspiration.

"I am," she smiled. "You are doing great."

"I am?" Eli questioned. "I feel like I'm being processed through a meat grinder."

"That's normal."

"Not for you, apparently. How can you be so relaxed?"

"I've already done many cleansings in my life, of different sorts," Angelina replied.

Eli winced as he felt his body temperature rise even further. It felt like the room was aflame. *I'm burning up*, he thought.

As though reading his thoughts, Somsak approached with a cold, wet towel. "Burn is good, but this help," he placed it on Eli's forehead. The towel offered instant relief. He closed his eyes and allowed himself to drift off into another dream state. In this one, he was not conscious of his surroundings but instead was absorbed into what felt like another realm.

Is this what heaven feels like? He wondered. Through a warm, bright light a human form started to appear. It did not take long for him to know that it was his father.

"Dad."

"Son. It is good to see you."

Eli's face became wet with tears as he said, "I thought I'd never see you again."

"Whether you see me or not, Eli, I will always be with you."

"I'm so sorry, Dad."

"Sorry for what?"

"I wasn't there when you died. I wasn't there much when you were alive, even. I missed out on a lot of experiences with you."

"Eli, I knew since the moment you were born that you were special. You had a higher purpose in this life—one that not many people would be able to handle as gracefully as you have. When I chose to become your father, I made a commitment to supporting you in that purpose, no matter the emotional sacrifices I might have to make."

"Wait, you chose to be my father?"

"Absolutely. Just as you chose me to be your father. We all have that choice before a baby is conceived. We chose each other. We are soulmates, don't you see?"

"Soulmates? I don't understand…"

"You think soulmates are just for romantic relation-ships? Think again, my son. Soulmates are partnerships of all kinds, brought into your life to lead you to your higher purpose. You and your mother are soulmates as well. And get this—every bully that has ever taunted you, every teacher you've ever had—they are all soulmates of yours as well. Everyone whose path you cross, Eli, was put there by design."

"Wow…"

"Wow is right," Robert laughed. "Now, why did you want to see me? What can I do for you?"

"Honestly, I'm not sure. I just wanted so desperately to tell you goodbye."

"You can tell me goodbye without seeing me, you know. But since we are both here, I want you to know that I had no regrets in my life, and I suggest that you don't in your life, either. The emotions of guilt, fear and regret only take away from your life force. Don't let them cloud your vision and steal your energy."

"I will try my best."

"And Eli?"

"Yes?"

"You were everything I ever wanted in a son and more. I am very proud of you. More than you'll ever know."

"Thanks, Dad."

"Now, I must go. I have important decisions to make about my next life.

"Will we see each other again?"

"We are soulmates, remember? We will cross paths again and again, my dear child. I may be your brother in another life, or perhaps even your son—or your daughter. Think about that one for a while," Robert winked.

"That is a little weird, I admit," Eli laughed. "But I look forward to knowing you again, in whatever form we take."

"One more thing, Eli. Remember, to die is really a celebration. It means we have accomplished what we were put on this earth to achieve. I am ecstatic that I have passed, and I hope you can share my joy. You may remember me with tears of pleasure and love, but please—not with pain."

"Okay, Dad. Thank you."

"No, thank you. You were one of the greatest gifts of my life. I love you with all my heart, and always will."

"I love you too, Dad."

Eli exited the other realm peacefully. He awoke feeling lighter and full of more life energy than ever before.

Eli and Angelina returned to L.A. a few days later feeling rested, more connected to each, and more connected to spirit. Sometimes Eli wondered if he had simply dreamed the experience of communicating with this dad, but he reminded himself that he was already communicating with Michael—a spirit from another realm—so why couldn't he have spoken with his father?

Since that experience, however, all of his dreams had become more vivid. He didn't use to remember his dreams hardly at all, and now he woke up each morning with a clear recollection of every dream he'd had the night before. Most of them were peaceful; he had dreams of being a boy again himself, playing on the farm. He had dreams about the future—ones that depicted the planet as healthy and all of its inhabitants happy.

But he also had dreams that disturbed him. He knew that Gemini was protecting him, and yet over the next few weeks he'd have dreams that its leaders were highly corrupt...aliens? He still wasn't sure what they were. They would shapeshift into non-human, reptilian-like beings. If he'd had the dream only once, he wouldn't have given it much thought but it was starting to become a reoccurring dream. He began to feel like there was a deeper message to the dream that he was missing.

After the fifth time he had the dream, Eli decided to ask Michael about it. He quietly rolled out of bed so as not to disturb Angelina, who was still sleeping. He shut the bedroom door behind him and stepped into the guest room down the hall.

"Michael?"

"Yes?" Michael appeared before him, seated in the armchair in the corner of the room.

"That was fast…"

"Always at your service. What can I do for you today?"

Eli described the dream he'd been having.

"Hmm…interesting," Michael responded.

"What do you make of it?" Eli asked.

"I'm not sure if I can tell you now…"

"Here we go again…" Eli sighed.

"Well, I will tell you this. Gemini is protecting your welfare, right?"

"Yes, that's what they told me. And I believe them."

"Good. You should believe them. They uphold their promises. But there's an ulterior motive to their offer you should know about."

"What is that?"

"You are under contract to reach a net worth of $40 billion in this lifetime, correct?"

"Yes…"

"That means they are under contract too. If they don't fulfill their end of the bargain, they will lose power."

"What power? Who is overseeing the contract?"

"That's what I can't yet tell you."

"Geez, Michael. Leave me hanging."

"I only told you what I did to help you understand that they may not be…who you think they are."

"Meaning?"

"For one thing, that they are not inherently good. Although they are protecting you, there is a dark side to the organization. They are part of a much bigger system—a system that humanity has been enslaved within for thousands of years and of which most people have no idea exists."

"Who is operating that system, Michael?"

"Let's just say, they are not of this world. And they are highly dangerous."

"Not of this world? What do you mean, like aliens or something?"

"Mmm…something like that."

"What, artificial intelligence?"

Eli could tell by Michael's reaction that he was onto something.

"You said it, I didn't. Let's just say, we're not alone. There is so much you don't yet know. And there's so much more you have yet to do—not just on this planet, but beyond. Now, I must go before I say too much."

With that thought, Michael left him. *But where does that leave me?* Eli wondered. He thought he'd understood so much…now he felt as though his education was just beginning.

I have so much left to do on this planet, and beyond. The words Michael had spoken hung in the air. *I know I have to earn another $20 billion. And I know I have to do something in response to the letter I received about more trafficking rings. And Mom and the farm—what am I supposed to do to help her out?*

Sufficiently overwhelmed, Eli thought a cold shower

might help his state of mind. He made his way back to the master bedroom. He could hear Angelina in the bathroom. *She's up*, Eli thought. *I wonder if I should tell her about these dreams and my chat with Michael?*

Just then, Angelina opened the bathroom door, emanating with a warm glow.

Eli was caught off guard by her natural beauty; he never grew tired of seeing his love naked.

"Good morning, baby," she smiled.

"Good morning," Eli replied, thinking he might set aside his thoughts and initiate making love instead.

"I wasn't talking to you," she winked.

"Huh?" For a moment, Eli actually considered who else could be in the room with them. Her smile and the placement of her hand on her belly, however, were enough to clarify what she had meant.

"No…are you? Are we…?" he stumbled to find the right words.

Angelina smiled and nodded. "We're going to have a baby." The words brought tears to both of their eyes.

Eli stood frozen; the news was joyful, but he was in shock. *A baby?!* His chest began to swell with pride, at the same time that his mind clouded with fear. Instantly, he felt responsible in a way he never had before.

Ohmigod. How can I protect a child in this crazy world? How will I find the time to be deeply present in my child's life? How do I keep from passing my karma onto him?

Angelina allowed him time to stand there and process before his thoughts finally rested on, *"We're going to have a baby!!!"* At that moment, he leaped into her arms and stroked her belly.

"Hello in there," he whispered. He then raised his gaze

Made in the USA
Columbia, SC
29 August 2018